DANIEL MOYANO was born in Buenos Aires in 1930 and died in exile in Madrid in 1992. When in Argentina he worked as a journalist and taught music at the Conservatory of La Rioja. He wrote seven novels including *The Devil's Trill*, also published by Serpent's Tail.

The FLIGHT of the TIGER

DANIEL MOYANO

Translated and with an Afterword by
Norman Thomas di Giovanni

Library of Congress Catalog Card Number: 93-87558

A catalogue record for this book can be obtained from the
British Library on request

First published in 1981 as *El vuelo del tigre* by
Editorial Legasa, Madrid

Copyright © 1981 by Daniel Moyano

Translation and Afterword copyright © 1995 by
Norman Thomas di Giovanni

This edition first published in 1995 by
Serpent's Tail, 4 Blackstock Mews, London N4 2BT and
180 Varrick Street, New York, NY 10014

Typeset in 10½ pt Garamond by CentraCet Ltd, Cambridge

Printed in Finland by
Werner Söderström Oy

CONTENTS

HAVING SCRAMBLED UP to the weathercock, Belinda looked out in amusement over the roofs of Hualacato, an Andean village lost somewhere amid the cordillera, the sea, and adversity.

The cat liked gazing at the moon as it changed colour in the shards of bottle glass set into the top row of bricks by the Aballays when, to keep out intruders, they had added another foot to the walls around their house. At this hour of night no sound of life could be heard; no insect, bird, or reptile seemed to exist. All these things were long since fixed in the cat's memory, and every night they drove her up to the weathercock, where she waited for events to unfold. It was an hour of safety, of continuing natural ceremonies, at a time when so much was changing in Hualacato and new things were afoot that did not figure in Belinda's memories of the night.

But they figured in old Aballay's, and he recounted them after his own fashion, embroidering tales while sticking to the basic facts, mixing animals and people – partly to get at the truth, partly to soften images that might have a detrimental effect on his memory.

When the percussionists come riding in on their tigers, Hualacato bends, its landscape changes. Time and crops are taken over, streets are closed or rerouted, roads no longer lead to their usual places. Hualacato shrivels up. In a kind of new architectural order that tourists babbling various tongues rush eagerly to photograph, house fronts gush tears from ailing cracks. Stonemasons using plumb lines find that the houses are like stalks of maize in the wind. Out of plumb, say the masons; and their plumb lines are taken away from them. Without which they fall back on a practised eye. Out of plumb, they say, no two ways about it. Then they are taken away. Out of plumb all the same, they just manage to say as they disappear behind massive doors, and buildings sag under unthinkable winds. Then the vicuñas stop mating, for everything has its response, old man Aballay would say. He had been skirmishing for forty years – after his own fashion, of course, from a wheelchair – making up stories.

In Hualacato everything is forbidden, but to hang on to joy people tune their instruments to a different pitch. As everyone knows, music is infinite. So when any given pitch is prohibited, the townspeople transpose to a lower or higher key. This way at least they can live in a world that parallels the real one. At the same time, so as not to lose their way, they retreat into old superstitions.

Dismounting their tigers, the percussionists proceed to take possession of everything. At home, only two places remain for Hualacateños – one for hunger, the other for cold. Water is bottled and sealed, and rain-water itself is collected by huge machines. Rain no longer falls in Hualacato.

This is not the first time percussionists have come. In the past forty years the old man has seen them arrive on horses or in lorries, always by night, from all the cardinal points, switching everything around and calling the north south, suspicious of everything, wilting flowers and people just by looking at them, staring at everything with eyes as sad as the world when the world feels ill. Always by night, their percussion, their racket, mingling with the sounds of life.

Hualacateños have sharp ears. They claim they can hear background sounds like out-of-step breathing, like percussive tapping. We can't sleep at night; it's as if tigers were sniffing at our doors. A lie, blare radios and television sets, the only tiger around here is the sickly specimen at the zoo. Then one day, all at the same time, like an orchestra, the Hualacateños pause and interrupt the course of life so as to catch those sounds in the background. In the streets and factories everyone muffles his or her own playing. Music stands are folded up. In the general silence, a mounting din. What sounded like heavy breathing is a rhythmless racket that assaults the ears.

Play, play something! bellow the percussionists up and down the streets, reproaching those who stand silent. They themselves clamber aboard their lorries, horns blaring, engines revving, even getting their dogs to bark. Despite which, the background cacophony can still be heard. Then patrols tramp the streets, shouting; night patrols, day patrols, in step and, according to need, howling, turning corners as if driven by the wind, running to drown out the din in this or that neighbourhood, running and barking like big black dogs to block out the din. If they won't play we'll make them, say the percussionists, and every night their lorries prowl the streets, stopping at corners, where men leap out and knock on doors, rounding up the silent. Whatever the cost, the percussionists will salvage their sounds.

Hualacateños who can still visit one another tap at the door with their fingertips while just making their voices heard. It's us, Juani and the kids, don't be afraid. For rapping with the knuckles would be too much like the percussionists' rat-a-tat-tat. While the inhabitants of Hualacato might mistake day for night they never mistake a door. They know them all by heart.

There is no longer any point in padlocking doors or adding a row or two of bricks to the walls around the houses. The percussionists get in anyway. The ironmongers have run out of locks, yet a good half of all Hualacato's houses have been taken over. You can tell by the small banners that fly from the rooftops to mark the presence of a percussionist.

The sick and feeble leave their lights on and do not bother to lock their doors. If this is the way it's going to be, let them come in; we're old and ailing, why hang on in this world? The simple-minded bolt their doors, prop tables and chairs and even the odd tree trunk against them; and they hang out a small sign as a reminder that a man's home is his castle. A man's home is no more than a thin shell, says old man Aballay, rubbing Belinda's fur the wrong way. We need other means of defence, he says, feeling a prickle of fear in his missing leg.

Everybody in Hualacato is in fear and trembling, and so is Belinda. In different houses, often at the same time, lights would go on, making them look like gaping wounds. There were cries and confusion, shadows leaping behind windows, a clatter as though men and objects were being smashed, white nightshirts wrenched from their beds, and a strong smell of turned earth, but not turned for sowing. The foul smell of the earth needlessly turned. Nobody plants seeds that way, much less by night, as far as the cat can remember. Hualacato looks ugly after dark, with gaping wounds going on and off. Ugly squeals of creatures in the woods, the crickets' chirr altering, birds chirping out of time, sleeping spiders trembling to see their seismographs leap, beetles seeking refuge in their carapaces – each and every one in terror. Creatures in their holes and nests, keeping clear of men but still in thrall to the body of men, still man's secret environment.

No gaping wounds in the distance now, everything in deep silence, as in Belinda's memories. The Aballays were asleep under their zinc roof, and now that the night was recovering its rhythm the cat would be asleep up on the weathercock had not a bird, a cricket, something alive and in her memory, stirred or groaned for some reason not part of its memory, and Belinda first heard, then saw, the lorry in the street, men leaping out of it and distributing themselves along doorways, walls, and windows, tapping at them with their batons, and the wounds flared up.

When Belinda saw that the man and his footsteps – in no particular hurry, almost bored – were headed for the house, she let out a caterwaul that filled the air with a virginal superstition. Her squawk went straight to the man's heart, touching forgotten fears. He pointed the baton in the direction of the cry but saw only the weathercock. By then Belinda was in the kitchen, hidden amongst the begonias, taking upon herself all the fears of the Aballays. From nearby walls and invisible trees other cats let loose a symphony of wailing. The Aballays flew from their beds. They're here, a woman shouted, and, half-dressed, the rest of them began scurrying about in the impossible light of that hour to converge on the kitchen. Last to arrive was the old man in his wheelchair, just as they heard the footfall of the man outside approaching either to knock at the door or to knock it down. The family looked from face to face, bidding each other farewell as if one of them was setting off on a journey. Embracing, they thanked each other for shared happiness and apologised for silly offences. At that hour the kids did not understand farewells and only wanted to be back in bed as soon as possible.

The man knocked at the door twice. Once inside, although it was the dead of night, he greeted them briskly, saying, Good morning, I'm the percussionist.

Well, well, well. So you're the musicians who refused to play, are you? No need for alarm, this is just routine. That's it, right up against the wall as if you're looking for a little spider. Stare at the wall long enough and a little spider'll show up. Stand still and no talking. All the rest of you, against the wall and don't move a muscle. Behave yourselves or there'll be no pudding, got that? Arm's length apart, please, eyes front, no talking, and just keep looking for the little spider.

He spoke as if he were devouring them, all the while frisking each in turn. They stood stock-still like rags hanging from the walls as he picked at small threads and turned over pockets. With one foot he turned over stones, exposing the faded shells of nocturnal insects to sunlight, then studying them with scientific interest while the bugs devoured their own saliva. You're the ones who won't bloody play. A pity. Are you all here? Is this all? Is this really all of you? No one under a bed? Or in the back room? On the roof? Anybody in the corners of the wardrobes? In the treetops? In the looms? In a cave? Behind doors? In the water tank? Or in a cabin trunk? Anyone in the empty site next door? In the ant hills? In the irrigation ditches? Or in the wood pile? Or under the chairs, the tables? Are there any garrets, cesspits, underground chambers? I don't want answers, I'm not asking questions. I'm only thinking aloud. I know everything. The baby in the cradle can stay there. The rest of you, keep looking for the little spider. One grandfather, one married couple, five children not counting the one in the cradle. A regular population explosion. Is this everyone? Is this absolutely everyone? I don't think so, the cat that climbs the weathercock isn't here.

Right, he said still gripping his baton. You can turn round now and leave the little spider for another time. I want you to look at me and get to know me. I'm not here to harm you. I've come to save you, not lose you. I've saved many families like you – and under worse circumstances. It's your duty to welcome me. Otherwise it will be my duty to set in motion operation number two, which I warn you is somewhat violent. As both radio and television have never tired of announcing, it was your voluntary duty to request a saviour. You failed to do so. Childish resistance. But on the other hand you refused to play, is that not so?

That you've not asked for a saviour places you in an awkward position. By the same token, am I to assume that like so many others in Hualacato you don't need a saviour? You'll have to prove that with deeds and show that you've no intention of rocking the boat and that you'll comply with all the regulations. This is *de facto*. Your ridiculous bit of resistance is over, and from this point on we talk. But you're going to play – about that you may rest assured.

Tonight I'll bed down anywhere. Tomorrow, when the new order begins, you'll provide a room for me with all the basics, since I'm likely to be with you for some time. My clothing and the papers and instruments I've brought guarantee the safety of everyone in this house – including my own, in view of the alarming number of saviours murdered by gutless criminals. I'm here to organise things, to teach you how to live in the real world, and to cure you of your foolish notions. Those notions have done you a lot of harm. I'm not a saint; I'm a practical man who's accepted reality. I'm a saviour because that's what I chose to be. Any of you can become a saviour if you want. But as of tomorrow you'll start playing, have no doubt about that.

You'll all go back to bed now and think over the questions you'll be allowed to ask tomorrow – barring anything silly or obvious, of course. For the moment, keep quiet. Get your toothbrushes, each of you, even if you've already cleaned your teeth. Some other time we'll have a talk about the correct use of the toothbrush. I'm sure the old man, for one, doesn't use his scientifically.

The Aballays finished dressing so that they could go to bed. Shorter ones first, they stood in a queue outside the bathroom door, eyes staring into space in search of small spiders.

'Can we at least know your name?' said the old man.

'My name's on the long side. Just call me Nabu.'

The percussionist sealed the door of every room and warned the family not to tamper with the seals without his permission. He set electric traps, stretched out on a cot, and turned off the light. All was going according to plan, except for the facts that the baby had not yet been born when action was initiated to take over the house and the cat had been overlooked by some witless clerk. Into his ears Nabu inserted some sort of apparatus that only he could hear and that would wake him up in a couple of hours. He began to relax and was soon fast asleep, when an outcry sent him into contortions, shrivelling him inside and out until he became a caricature of himself, a scrap of wrinkled paper, with his hair falling about his eyes. His face looked as if it was painted on a deflating balloon.

Nabu would never have believed that so many cats could break out caterwauling at the same time. Dishevelled, defenceless, putting himself together like the pieces of a jigsaw puzzle, Nabu rushed to the patio. The cats cried as if they knew their wails would grate on his nerves. Almost weeping with anger, he threw a hand grenade. Just when it was all going so well. In the flash, he saw walls and trees infested with ears and whiskers. Eviscerated in mid-air, disarticulated, cats pattered down on the zinc roof like big raindrops, trickled to the bottom of the slope, clattered into the gutter, and spilled to the ground. Cats fallen from grace were falling from the sky.

When a once more tranquil Nabu returned to his cot, from the shadows of one of the room's many shelves, Belinda, camouflaged amongst the begonias, first put out a whisker, then an ear, and listened for a considerable length of time to the percussionist's fitful breathing. When the rhythm of his chest steadied and he was asleep, she stuck out her whole head. Fur bristling, Belinda stared at Nabu with big yellow eyes.

2

OF THOSE FIRST DAYS of salvation single images remain, moving shapes, scars added to nature. Freshly shaven and smelling of lavender, Nabu sits on a table, legs dangling over the edge, ringing a tiny bell to waken the family. He sits there ringing that same little bell while other bells fastened round his neck tinkle and Nabu orders the Aballays to queue up according to height. Towels and toothbrushes in hand, they have four minutes to wash and then all of you straight back Nabu said, Nabu says, Nabu will go on saying for ever. Even if you shut your eyelids tight he will always be there. Lift your arms higher, stretch your neck, and rotate your head. Never had much exercise, have you? And reading out sermons, morality, healthy habits, bloody hell, those who refused to play but once played other things. I know the dates and places you played only a short while ago, things that are still fresh, and many more if we were to go back. Before losing your leg you played trains, shops, public monuments, and sacred symbols. It's all down in black and white, and your son accompanied you. That's in writing too. Making up trains and monuments that did not exist then, in a tone of voice that created them and made you believe. His voice was not strident. He shouted with his face, especially his eyes, and they reached heights no voice could ever reach. And now all of you to your rooms, he says in the same voice in which he mentioned trains set on fire, and start thinking hard about the things you've played. Black pasteboard covers the windows, so there's no knowing what's outside. Maybe figs will ripen in the garden. Scars. The postman comes, and Nabu says, I'll read every letter first, of course. Foolish to think in these circumstances we can let you communicate freely with people out there. Can I go and do some shopping? asks Coca like a simpleton. Smiling, Nabu lets it pass and purveyors arrive with their boxes, factory remnants, lipids and starches, no sugar today either, the shortage is terrible. But at least Grandad can go out in the garden or patio and bask in the sun. That's very dangerous, Nabu says. They're areas of potential conflict, with stones and holes, he could fall and break his other leg. The doorbell rings. People bearing more regulations and instruments, Nabu signs, and they leave. Each item that arrives means more time, like the slip of paper from the factory where Cholo works. For as long as necessary you've been granted the special leave I requested for you, images, images, and you can go back to your rooms without a word. The endless night, sounds out there, chickens flapping their wings, the rumble of thunder but no rain, then everything silent, patrols treading on cotton, and sunrise again, with the bells and lavender, one, two, the gym and how to use your toothbrush correctly, another day and you haven't told me anything important yet (they're all scars), and you, take that dress off, it's not right for you, but it's very warm in here, you take that off immediately, and Coca goes and undresses while Julito sucks his dummy and Sila answers questions in one of the rooms and Kico awaits his turn, staring up at the ceiling, and the old man trims a cannula to make a pipe. And Nabu rushing about looking for more files, saying what's *that*, taking old Aballay's penknife away from him. In my view a penknife's a sharp instrument, says Nabu. Why wasn't it declared when we drew up the inventory? Some things get overlooked, says the old man, bereft of penknife and cannula. Nabu's apprenticeship. Scars. Clocks and watches stopped and banned. What time is it, please? asks Cholo foolishly. You are incommunicado, says Nabu, laden with watches and handbags. Must be night, says Cholo under his breath. Can't be, says Coca. So little time has passed. You think it's night because it's probably cloudy. Across the room, Nabu opens the front door, scribbles his signature, receives more parcels, tends to the postman, and two or three days later further correspondence will arrive. He has no time to read any of it. Aunt Francisquita writes, saying next to nothing, only that we must have faith, kisses for the children, and Carlos sends his regards. Coca is in the kitchen peeling potatoes, and Nabu is in the next room questioning her husband. I never played those things, says Cholo. We seem to be talking about different times, so we'd better get this straight. You never played them. Do you think I don't know that before playing them you never played them? It's easy enough for you to say you never played them. But I mean *later*, I'm asking you about after you played them, in which case it'd be a lie to say never. Because you have played, and here are the dates. You know very well I never played, this is all a fabrication, I never played, I wasn't playing then. Maybe you weren't playing, but you were going to play. Were you going to play or had you already played? Had you to play or having played were you now about to play? Because had you, you would have been having to. Isn't that so? I don't under-stand, sir. You had to play, you all had to, I've the dates and specific places. Had you to have had or had you having had? Maybe you hadn't then but would have had, isn't that right? Had you or hadn't you had whatever it was or had you had whatever it had been? I wasn't it, not me. Ah, so then it was, hadn't it? Why did you deny having done whatever it was, then? It's plain you had to play, or rather that you did. I hadn't played, I didn't. Lies, falsehoods, just now you said you hadn't played what you had, or rather had had. I don't know whatever was, but I wasn't. You hadn't because you already had. It's becoming gradually clearer. You had had, hadn't you, yes or no? No, I hadn't had. Would you have or had you had? I want straight answers. No, I would not have had. Damn it, you wouldn't have had if what. You wouldn't have had or not had what was – that is, whatever it had been. No, sir, I'd none of whatever had been had, I know nothing whatever about having had. Come on, you must have had what it was if whatever it was was what you had had. Would you have whatever it had been? Hiv you or hav you or hud you? Wull you hav hud huving? No, I've neither hiv nor hud. Then you huv also whatever hiv hud, and this makes matters worse, because it means, then, that you hiv, had, huv, and hudded. Have you not, then? They're shapes, scars. And Kico stares at the ceiling awaiting his turn, and at nine a whistle blows and they all go to bed and sleep won't come and lightning in the windows announcing rain that won't come. It's Nabu's flares looking for cats on the walls, scars, everything sticking in the mind, to the skin, scars like the five continents with their seas. At last a bit of joy when Nabu pins up a calendar and we find out what day it is. Today's Sunday, says Nabu, so that we can start counting the days again. How wonderful, the old man says, and the saviour smiles with satisfaction. He has given us time, scars. But their time isn't calendar time, they have their own numbers and count in a different way, Cholo says. Their numbers are the hours locked up in a room and having to ask permission for everything, Nabu pacing up and down at mealtime and reading out his sermons, and the subject for today is that paradoxical thing, violence. And in the afternoon, question time. Today it's Kico's turn, let's see what it was, anyway we all were, Nabu has already solved it, while we try to think up cheerful things, paring our nails is one, a possible boyfriend for Sila is another, our compadre's son, not the brightest of lads but bound to get better in his own way. We used to go up into the hills berry-picking and cutting firewood. We'd drop in on Juanjo for coffee, on Aunt Céfira for New Year's Eve, on Yeyo to look at his ears of maize. We used to. Now Nabu gives us a calendar the way the corner grocer used to at the end of the year. You've never exercised, have you? And now each to your own room without a word, Nabu's whistle and bells in the morning, Nabu's permission to take a bath, Nabu reading letters he hands over to us the next day, lipids and starches and no sugar for anything, never a glimpse of the sun, not even the children, how nice to be in the patio right now, maybe leaves are falling from the vine, maybe they are just opening out, how nice it would be to stand out in the patio now, it looks like a wonderful day, but only the percussionist knew that a fine rain was falling. Scars, all scars.

3

THE PERCUSSIONIST GAVE them a two-hour break indoors. You can talk, have a wash, cut your nails; you can draw, weave, make paper cut-outs; the kids can play London Bridge, hide-and-seek, or ring a ring o' roses while the grown-ups play board games. But no noise, no shrieking voices. I've work to do, so don't get on my nerves.

And he locked himself up in the middle of the L-shaped house in the room with the big windows, where he could tend to his job and still keep an eye on the two parts of the L. *Click* went the percussionist's eyes whenever anyone got a glass of water, *click* when anyone went to or left the bathroom, *click* if by mistake someone set a foot out of bounds. *Click*, at every turn the Aballays were snapped by Nabu's eyes from there in the middle of the L. Nabu's face, Nabu's body always on the lookout. On the way to the bathroom you'd tell yourself no, I won't look at him, but at a given moment you lifted your eyes, you couldn't help it, your eyes went up and you had to look at him just as his eyes came up from his papers or maps and went *click*. On your way to and fro he was there every time, *click*, sitting or standing or whatever his position his eyes always went *click*.

What did the percussionist look like? His face was

nondescript; you couldn't say his eyes were like this, his nose like that, or anything about his hair, chin, eyebrows, or hands. He was and he wasn't. He was there, where he had somehow always been. He was there now, but that included before and after. What he had for a face was more like a scar of some kind. Of the fangs of a dog bite when we were kids, no actual scar remains – not of a dog bite, anyway, more like a blotch left by a burn or a scrape. It's a mark. Of Nabu you could say you remember when he was not there, even though he was always there. As the little spider, no doubt, was always there, though we never found it.

What about writing him a letter? said Coca, all in a fluster. She realised the others were giving her a patronising look. The idea! OK, no big deal. Not a letter to him exactly but one he can pass on to someone else. Or why not a letter to him? Silly as it sounds, at least we know him, right? I've written dozens of letters for people who don't know how to write, asking for things they don't have, and sometimes they get them. Don Floro's crutches came by post – a single letter, and they arrived at once.

How about looking at some snaps? Where are the boxes? Remember the times when it rained or was too cold and we couldn't go out and we'd spend hours poring over snapshots and eating fritters? Aunt Francisquita's wedding pictures were lovely. Whenever people stayed too long and we got bored we'd dig out the old photos. Is this you? It's plain you've always been a strong man, said our visitors, bored to tears. It was Cholo, but we never told them. Not that they were interested. Remember the Carnival snaps? We had loads of them. The Three Musketeers, but I can't recall who they were, a lot of Devils with tiny mirrors sewn into their capes, Cholo as Ali Baba – I remember that one – and those Apache dancers, Kico and Sila, though you wouldn't recognise them now. And the pictures of the kids when they were small: their First Communion wearing sailor suits, their first teeth, and their first school uniforms. And the ones taken the time we went to the capital, the lights, the train, the station and everything, when Sila got cross and didn't want her photo taken because she couldn't get anyone to buy her everything she set her heart on. Sure, we might hunt for the boxes and look at the snapshots. It'd be a lot less boring than playing board games. OK, but it's not raining and we've neither photos nor fritters. What do you mean we have no photos? He's got them, didn't you know? The photos and the letters. They were the first things he locked up in that desk of his.

Never mind, we practically know them by heart. If each of us remembers something we could reconstruct them. How about Sila's birthday party, say? Anyone remember those pictures? A silly fifteen-year-old flirt. There's one of her under the grape arbour, cutting the cake and looking like an idiot. Face all pimply and Bocha glued to her, his teeth sticking out as if he were trying to kiss her. Why don't you stop all that nonsense and help me write this letter? There was another of Grandad on the day we got Belinda, so sweet with that bow we tied on her, the two of them together looking cheerful behind their whiskers. And there's a snap of poor little Tite too. None of you ever knew him. He came between Sila and Kico. He was four. One of those summer diarrhoeas, insects, flies.

Any of you remember Aunt Francisquita's wedding? You wouldn't, you were too young – even if you are in the pictures – but Kico and Sila were old enough and they're sure to. How could they, they spent the whole day setting off squibs and bothering the neighbours, who complained about the noise. Rather than a wedding, I think what was being celebrated was the fact that Aunt Francisquita had finally made it. She was over forty. OK, don't exaggerate; she had a few wrinkles but she wasn't that bad. She had her hair tinted walnut. She liked wearing white, remember? She appeared at the end of the road. Look, here comes Aunt Francisquita to visit us, and there she was in the middle of the dirt road in a white dress, her suitcase full of toys. You remember those musical tops? We still have one, but its string is broken. How did she manage to marry Uncle Carlos, when he was so young? What's the matter with you all, talking about Aunt Francisquita as if she were old and ugly? She was not old. And on the night of the wedding, in her veil and bouquet of orange blossoms, she looked like a princess. Yes, but the women guests went up and down whispering, saying a white wedding was ridiculous at her age. Her half-length train really suited her. The others were green with envy. They were the same age as she but fat and hairy. Naturally, you won't find them in any of the photos. They refused to let a camera near them.

Who was there at the party? Well, Yeyo, who brought the maize pasties, and his children of course, who were always climbing trees. There was Juanjo, uttering difficult words as usual and scolding the twins, who never understood a thing he said. No, that was another photo. The twins didn't play football at Aunt Francisquita's wedding. That's true, in this snapshot they look so squeaky clean. What about Lucho and Aunt Céfira – weren't they there? Of course they were there; the party was held at their place. Aunt Francisquita had a room in a boarding house, and Céfira and Lucho lent her their house for the reception. Over a hundred people fitted into the first patio alone, and there was acres of room at the back where the kids could run about. There's a picture of Marcelina at that party, reciting poetry. Aunt Marcelina was so pretty. What do you mean *was*? She still lives round the corner. That's true, time does fly. It's as if Aunt Marcelina were no longer with us.

And the house? Does anyone really remember the house? There couldn't have been a better place for Francisquita's wedding party. She used to stay there when she came to Hualacato. There was a lemon tree in the patio, and I think a walnut tree too. No, I mean what was the house like on the outside. There's a really good picture of the front of it. You hardly ever noticed the front; you just went inside. Let me think, was it plain brick or plastered? I don't know, but it was painted. The colour, I can't remember. It had a doorbell, of course, like any other house. Did it have a sloping roof? Maybe not, but the photo would tell. No, it must have, because whenever it rained and you looked out of the window all you saw was a sheet of water coming down over the eaves; then, when the rain stopped, the drips left a row of small holes in the ground below. The inside's easier. On the wedding day, under the grape arbour, the patio was laid out with tables. White grapes or red? Both, I think. Aunt Francisquita arrived a few weeks earlier carrying a suitcase full of things for her wedding – cloth for her trousseau and veil, and a little basket for flowers. Everything – thread, cloth, buttons, trimmings – was bought in the capital. Cost an arm and a leg, of course. She couldn't sew the gown herself, she was so short-sighted, and no spectacles would do for her. So Céfira sewed everything. The petticoats were like ball gowns, embroidery and lace everywhere, and everything pure white for Aunt Francisquita's first night. The two shut themselves up for a whole week in the room with the handloom before they could make up their minds how to cut the cloth for the gown. There wasn't enough for a long gown with a full train. Aunt Francisquita wanted something calf-length and a long train, but Aunt Céfira said with her bandy legs that was out. They couldn't get it right. The width of the bloody cloth was all wrong. At some point, weeping and sweating at the same time, Aunt Francisquita thought she'd never get married. Everything was coming to grief because the cloth wasn't wide enough, and she saw herself growing old in a boarding house, on her bedside table a yellowing photograph of Carlos, who ultimately married someone else.

Let Francisquita be and listen to this, please. I want to know if I'm getting it right. *Dear Sir, I am writing to you with all due respect to explain as a mother what we are really like, since as things stand you may never get to hear us, not of course out of neglect but owing to the enormous amount of work you have. I wanted to inform you that it was not by playing what you said that my father-in-law lost his leg but . . .*

When they came to an agreement they found themselves in a terrible rush because there were only four days to go. Coca went round to see them a few times. The room was hot, and the two dripped sweat. Unable to work in their dresses, they'd stripped down to their petticoats. Their hair was in streaks, and not wanting to drop their scissors even for a minute they put on no make-up. And the whole time they gabbled about lingerie and the house Carlos had bought for his bride. It was a surprise. No one had seen it or knew where it was. And the whole place a muddle of linen, crystal, coffee spoons, and cups. What about the dress? The trickiest part, you can't even see in the picture. They began by cutting a pattern in paper. It was Aunt Céfira's first crack at a bridal gown and she wasn't about to take scissors directly to such expensive material. They worked out the idea from a magazine cover, pinned to the flyblown wall, that showed a beautiful girl – young, of course, and with a slim waist. Draped in her paper frock, Aunt Francisquita turned round and round, while Céfira took pins from her mouth and stuck them into the hem and drew chalk lines where seams and tucks were needed. Then her scissors went dancing round the hemline. The dress wasn't finished until the wedding day. The witnesses were already there, pacing up and down and glancing at their watches, while the two women sewed on the last details. Carlos sat by, calm as could be, as if none of it had to do with him. Somebody dashed out to collar a photographer. When the gown was pressed and a few of the guests had arrived, Aunt Francisquita, who wasn't the least bit nervous – or fat, as everyone claims – hung it up and stood gazing at it. Céfira told her to get into the bath and stop wasting time like a fool or she'd never get dressed. Not batting an eye, Francisquita opened her suitcase, took out a small box of trimmings, and showed them to Céfira, who'd know where they should go. All that went out with the Ark, Céfira said. By now she was a nervous wreck herself and dropped a handful of spangles and sequins on the floor.

Once the bride was dressed, Carlos was let in puffing on a cigar. You can see it in the snap, hanging over the edge of the table. He loved the toque and veil but said nothing about the embroidered bodice or the pleats, the prettiest things in the picture. *Playing what you said but farming. He wanted to quit his job at the ministry, where he served coffee. He had a lease on some uncultivated land and as a result of an accident felling trees he had his leg amputated. There are witnesses to all this. As to Cholo, sir, we grew up together so I know him well. We learned to become weavers at the same time, and I can assure you he has not played what you say either. Had he ever played them, I would know because he never keeps anything from me. You may ask about my husband at the factory. He has never been ill or missed a day's work, not for years. As for Kico and Sila, I swear they are model children who have never . . .* I don't think he even glanced at the bodice or at anything else. Aunt Francisquita was just one big blob to him. Then none of you ever saw him reading the paper with a magnifying glass? On the night of the wedding party Aunt Francisquita, who in spite of everything saw better than he did, slyly handed him things or placed an ashtray at his elbow. Otherwise every time he reached for a piece of bread or a glass of wine he would have stuck his hand in the cake. Does anybody remember her place, which she did up like a boarding house? That's what a twit she was. Well, I didn't call round all that much, finding them a bit bland. The house is on a little hill. Lots of geraniums in front, big picture windows, and inside everything just so, a hall-stand where you were supposed to hang your hat, a mat to wipe your feet on before you came in, and all of it staid, like them, small coffee cups on little doilies, a napkin to wipe your mouth. Exactly like a boarding house.

The snaps I like best are of the snow. Have you ever seen the one of Grandad in a snow drift up to his pipe? We took those on the hill. It was a rare sight, cactus draped in snow. Yes, but the one with the pipe wasn't on the hill. How could I have got up the hill in a wheelchair? When the rest of you left, I went out into the patio to smoke a nice pipe. I loved being outdoors when it snowed. For years no snow had fallen in Hualacato. It was the first time for you lot, the second for me. Many people were ruined by it, losing all their livestock. Sila, who was very small, had the silly idea it was raining sugar. The photo was taken by Aunt Francisquita. She came rushing home to announce that it was snowing – as if nobody knew. She took several of me but only one came out. The rest were blurred. I took the one of her in the snow, as white as on her wedding day. I can still picture her.

The ones of Tite didn't come out at all. In those days most snapshots came out blurred. We didn't have the cameras you have today. Or very dark. Whenever we looked at photos and one of Tite came up I'd hide it at the bottom of the box. I'd turn it face down and mark it with a cross so's not to look at it again. The worst was showing photos to visitors and having to answer who he was. It didn't come out, it's all blurred, they should never have printed it. But he's a sweet boy, they'd say just to say something, and at the point I was about to turn the photo over and go on to the next one, saying no more, your mother would begin explaining. That's Tite, he came between Kico and Sila, he was four, the flies, it's a miracle the others are alive. I didn't have it in me to destroy them, so I'd hide them, but they always turned up, mixed in with the others. There'd be Tite, in the middle of the Carnival pictures, blowing up a balloon; in the middle of the snow he never saw there he'd be with his balloon. She just couldn't part with them. I'd hide them in the oddest places, but she always found them and they'd be back in the box. I'm glad Nabu's got hold of them now. It's just as well they got lost. This is why at first I didn't like the idea of our looking at snapshots. I'd rather have played a board game or cut out paper birds. That's more fun. Why spend our break looking at bygone things? You have to be bored to death for that – or have a strong stomach. Now that all the days seem cold or rainy – and with nothing to do – you think what a good chance to look at the old snapshots. And then the ones with the candles. They're the worst, and I don't mean they came out blurred. They're kept together, tied up with a piece of string. In black and white

nothing looks better than candles. Even when the photographer isn't all that good, they still come out in focus. I
could never get through the lot of them; after a while, I
just turned them face down. Over the years I'd look at
them a few at a time. A glance and turn them over. I never
saw the actual candles. I went off that day, far away. If I
never saw the event itself, how could I bear it in a
snapshot? I don't know who took them. One or two came
out in the paper, Tite in a forest of candles, illustrating an
article on summer diarrhoea – an endemic disease, they
said. You shouldn't be upset, this isn't an everyday death,
this is the death of a little angel, the old women said. You
must eat and drink, invite your friends, tell jokes; a little
angel's death is different, everyone knows that. It's not
death, there's no limbo or anything, he's gone straight to
heaven. Really, it's not a bad superstition. Don Floro's
kids came and sang carols, as if he lay in a manger, and the
house was full of flowers and priests. Flies swarmed round
him the same as when he was alive. I learned all that
looking at the pictures a few at a time whenever we had
visitors or it rained. I'd been with Tite before the end and
could tell from the nurses' faces what was going to happen.
It was late, they were male nurses and haggard and they
shook their heads and one said, I'm sorry, it's not good,
it's a case of, and they uttered complicated words. I was
by his side just as dawn broke, the birds were already
singing, and he looked much smaller in that big bed there
at the casualty ward or first-aid room or whatever it was.
The nurses complained they had no cotton wool and were
opening empty boxes. Too hot this summer, a timely rain
would have cleared the whole thing up. Tite grew more
and more still. After that he turned into someone blowing
up balloons in snapshots, someone who came between
Kico and Sila, though he's nowhere now and only comes

on rainy or very cold days when you can't go out. All of a sudden he's there at Aunt Francisquita's wedding reception just as they're about to cut the cake. What's his connection with the party or anything else? None.

Well, I think you've gone too far with Tite's story. You'll spoil our break. Another minute or two and we'll be back with Nabu. That's like Monday morning at the factory all over again. Let's return to Aunt Francisquita or look at some of the others. There must be another boxful. No, let's leave Aunt Francisquita in peace. Right now I'd rather go through Tite's pictures once and for all and tear them up or get rid of them. I've always been afraid of them. But just this minute I can do it, I can face them. I can erase all the crosses I put on the back of them and for the first time look at them in a natural way. I'm not hiding them any longer. If you're going to sit down and look at pictures, then look at them all. Tite's a fact the same as all this is a fact. After all, he showed us how to die. His was the first death in the family. I hate the word but I'm beginning to live with it. Whichever way you look at it, it's ugly – every last letter of it. There's an A in death and an A in Nabu. Changing one letter and adding another, death could be health. Depending on how you look at it. There's an A in health and an A in Nabu. It was healthy that Tite never knew Nabu. Tite's dead and buried, and here we are playing with letters. Finally dead and buried – dead, anyway. Get out all the pictures. Now that Nabu's here I want to see them all. Maybe they'll be good for something, maybe they'll help me face up to what I was trying to forget. Soon it will be Monday. A as in Nabu. Doorbell, Monday, death. Nabu is, Nabu was, Nabu will be, and in the snapshots Tite in the throes of death, an endemic disease, no air to breathe, asking for help, not knowing he's in the middle of Carnival, no idea why everyone's in fancy dress, how the snapshots got mixed up. He's leaving because he does not understand, he's leaving on time, led out by the flies and endemic disease, someone snapping pictures of him at the little angels' wake. No need to be sad, they go straight to heaven. Why be here when at any moment now Nabu will show up with his verb tenses?

True enough, we shouldn't mix up all the photos. Tite and such will go in one box. If she could live for ever in a photo, Aunt Francisquita wouldn't like to be mixed up with Tite. And he wouldn't like appearing in Carnivals, out of sorts and out of focus. He went his own way and knows nothing of Aunt Francisquita, for he never got to know her. We should put all Tite's pictures in one separate box, and if anyone wants to look at them they can. Tite's still with us; the pictures don't bother me now. I hadn't realised it until Nabu came. Before that, they were snapshots of a dead person. I turned them over to avoid them, like someone avoiding a cemetery. With Nabu here, I see something else. Tite died a natural death. I know a natural death can be ugly too. But it's different, even if it was caused by an endemic disease. Sometimes when I feel I can't go on, when I can't take any more, when there's nothing to look back on or look forward to and everything's dark, I think about Tite in a natural way. In that black void there's something; Tite's there, just as in a very dark photo you can still make out a figure, *as for Kico and Sila, I swear they would never play anything. They are weavers, like the rest of us. Let me assure you, sir, as a mother and citizen of Hualacato* ... Has anyone noticed we have no photos of Yeyo? How can that be when he was there at every party? True, he was, but he was the one who had the camera. Yes, he did take most of them. Bocha taught him how to develop them. They'd lock themselves in the darkroom with their liquids and a bottle of gin and keep at it to the last drop. How many snaps do you suppose were developed with gin? Remember how they always came out of the darkroom singing?

I can't remember a thing about Yeyo. How can I when he isn't in any of the pictures? Well, first thing every morning Yeyo would step out into the sun and inspect his maize patch. It's what he most loved doing. The thing about Yeyo was the way he'd say, when asked how his maize was doing, 'sprouting nicely'. He never ate it. Not even once. He just loved watching it grow, and he knew the plants one by one. They were all different, he claimed. And this says a lot about Yeyo too. He gave every last ear away. He'd suddenly appear on your doorstep and say, here's some corn on the cob, and no bugs in it. That we had maize of our own meant nothing to him. And off he'd ride on his bicycle. To him, the ears of maize were something left over from the field, a little bundle wrapped in a husk. The way blind people must imagine what they can't touch. That's what he was giving away. It's hard to recall what he was like with no photos. We really loved Yeyo, even though we don't remember exactly what he looked like. Yeyo was something that was always there. He never missed a party. Wherever you went, you asked, Yeyo here yet? And the answer was always the same. Course, he's somewhere around. And as soon as you turned your head, there he was. It was wonderful. Yeyo's just the way his ears of corn were to him. Or even better, the way we'd picture him if we were blind. I don't think we'll ever see Yeyo again.

The rest are pictures of distant relatives, cousins we hardly know and who live far away. Roque, for one. No one knows who he is. Roque, what a name! Could anyone say Uncle Roque? Sounds awful. Or my cousin Roque.

But I think this Roque isn't a cousin or anything else for that matter. It's hard to explain exactly what he is to us. Nobody remembers him except for one woman I know, but here's his photo with what he wrote on it, to my dearest Aballay relatives, affectionately, Roque. A studio portrait, no less, with a label on it, Light and Shadow Studios, between covers and protected by a sheet of tissue paper so that Roque's picture will last for ever, bloody hell, too big to fit in any box so that wherever you put it part of this Roque always sticks out in his hired suit, looking like minor royalty. He's standing beside some piece of furniture, fingers just touching it to show off all his rings, not sure what to do with the other hand, and before the camera clicked he puts the free hand on his chest, Napoleon-style, above the watch-chain that runs out of his waistcoat pocket. Trousers beautifully pressed, look at the crease. And his cape, my goodness, and wing collar! And hat like a banking mogul. To say nothing of the bookshelves, giving him an intellectual air. Erasmus, Arthur Schopenhauer in big letters. Despite his face, Roque must be fairly brainy. Everything hired, of course. Studios like that hired you everything – the furnishings, the clothes on your back. I'd love to see him coming out of the place, no rings, no cape. Poor Roque. He was in love with Sila for quite a while, wasn't he? Not a week passed without one of his letters. Special delivery. Not exactly love letters. He kept skirting the subject, never quite daring to bring it up. A grown-up man. He said he knew me from a group photo sent him by some relative of ours and wanted me to send him a picture of me all by myself. All his letters ended, please don't forget your photo. I wrote back, naturally, but when he sent his picture I stopped, in spite of what he called his honourable intentions. Roque put his foot in it.

Remember our postcards? The best ones were Lucho's when they went to the seaside. Impressive, he said. Skyscrapers almost coming out of the waves. But remember that friend or compadre or whatever he was of Grandad's? The one who really got around and sent us postcards from cities all over the world with wonderful stamps on them. As a matter of fact, he's never set foot outside Hualacato. He was a coffee man at the ministry, just like me. We got postcards there all the time from countries wanting to sell us things. Publicity. We'd keep them for a while, then they'd end up in the dustbin. After I left the ministry, my compadre began collecting them. He'd rub out what was written on them and for fun he posted them to friends. He was always sending his regards from Oslo or Tokyo. The great thing about him were his carrier pigeons. If they'd let him, he'd have had his own private post office with all Hualacato. He has a pigeon for every person he knows.

Let me assure you, sir, as a mother and citizen of Hualacato, that neither of the two was ever mixed up in anything odd. Of the others, who are still very small, there is nothing to say. Sir, I humbly beg you, that's as far as I've got, what do you think? I don't know what else to ask of him. Well, I do, but as it's nothing you can really ask for it's as if there was nothing else. What I mean is, you have to ask for everything. Can't you see you can't ask him for anything? Apart from permission to go to the bathroom or whatever, there's nothing else to ask for. To begin with, he should be asked to leave. But his whole existence is tied up with being here. How can we ask him to go away? OK, it's the first thing we should ask him but the last he'd grant even if he were to grant anything. Besides being tied up with being here, he exists because he takes things. Snapshots and letters are only a small part of it. Nabu's taken everything. We can talk now because he's given permission. He's taken our words too. There's nothing we can ask of Nabu, mainly because we can't ask him to leave. Since he's here to take things away from us, what can we ask him for? Lower your voices, be careful, he's looking this way. Keep quiet, kids, and try to look sad. Though he claims the opposite, what most soothes his nerves is our sadness. Any time he hears me singing, he whips his head round and says, do you think you're in any position to be singing? If I were you I wouldn't, so please shut up. Not that I really sing. Doing the housework, I hum to myself, but my mouth's not open. It's a habit, and I told him so. Then you'll just have to break your habit, that's what he said to me. What can he be reading, I wonder. Letters, can't you see? He keeps letters in the red folder. Do you suppose he has any of Cachimba's letters? What's wrong, why are you so scared? Because he's questioned each one of us about Cachimba. He asks about him every time we're questioned. I said of course I knew him, he's from Huala-cato. Everybody knows Cachimba. Knowing him must be dangerous. No, we haven't any pictures of Cachimba. Letters, either – luckily. Maybe a Christmas card. But even a card might prove dangerous. He must be a threat to them, I can tell by the way Nabu says Cachimba, the look that comes over him when he says Cachimba. It's as if he meant to say something else but Cachimba comes out. Which is like saying horseshit or cockroach or criminal. He squashes the name with his foot whenever he says it; it turns his stomach. Even to me the word Cachimba means something else now. It used to have a nice sound. Now it scares me. What can poor Cachimba have done, I wonder. They must be tracking him with dogs. Those dogs roaming all night, they must have let them sniff one of Cachimba's shirts. If he's run away, they must have sent the dogs up into the woods. Please, keep your voices down and don't mention the name Cachimba. We'd better keep talking about the snapshots. Let's talk about something pleasant. I like the pictures taken at the zoo, the little monkeys jumping about, the bear always begging. *Kree, kree,* cry the monkeys. Do you know why Aunt Francisquita married so late? Mourning. One day she was boiling a big vat of dye out in the back patio and the very next day she's all in black. That was the first time, and it wasn't so bad – only four years. Then, in the last four months, when she was in half-mourning, a closer relative dies, and this time it's six years. So all the new clothes she's been making go into the vat all over again and she stays indoors. Of course, when she finally got out of mourning she was a bit long in the tooth. Have we any photographs of Avelina? I can't remember. Avelina, of course we do. That could prove risky too. If he found out Aunt Avelina is Cachimba's wife, we might be landed in it. Well, we have some. In one she's by a honeysuckle bush. Yes, I've seen it too, but some time ago. Maybe it got lost. No, it's in the tin box. I saw it a short time ago. Then we can be in serious trouble. If he comes across it he'll think we're all Cachimbas. Careful, here he comes. Keep still, kids. Like in the snaps.

4

A PRESENCE NOT UNLIKE that of the potted begonias, whose green leaves are mottled red in their centre. The more they are kept in the dark, the larger the area of red. It's best to store the pots in dim light so as to strike a balance in the coloration. In full sunlight the leaves turn bright green; in the dark they go completely red and die of asphyxia.

A presence not unlike when, switching off the light, you realise a strange animal is loose in the house. An unseen being, breathing, stalking, appearing you never know when. In complete darkness, this vermin throbs, bright red, verging on asphyxia, its colour and smell spreading from it as the asphyxia sets in round its edges. A presence whose colour spreads to the Aballays, in their beds with red spots advancing over their backs, clogging their lungs, pushing up into their noses and mouths, which are already peppered with tiny red spots and gasp for air.

Cholo is aware for the first time that his body is one more thing that can be taken from him. A desire, a need, comes over him to hold on to his chest to keep it from being taken away. Already his legs feel lost, apart from him, far away. His arms are useless, struggling to get free of him, but he won't let go of them, knowing he'll need them to hold on to his chest when they come to take it away from him. He breathes through his mouth and nose at the same time, desperate for air. In the snapshot of him by the honeysuckle, Aunt Avelina is gulping down all the air. Aunt Avelina who in Nabu's mouth, when he comes across her, becomes Uvelina. So there's an Unt Uvelina, then, is there?

Studying the red spots on his back, Coca hears Cholo's rasping breath. Cholo seems about to perish. The spots now girdle him, reaching round his stomach. It's ringworm. He touches his back, ringworm, at the same moment recalling Avelina's photo and the tin box, a tea caddy, Mandarin Brand Tea or some such, a Chinese box depicting dragons or cheongsams, a rubber band replacing the broken metal clasp, the box gone astray in the house and its contents of snapshots lost. Cholo suddenly shuts his eyes to keep out the sight of Nabu, who comes tripping along, the box in hand.

We've never set eyes on her; we have no idea who she is; the wind must have blown it in, Coca rasps. A badly developed or poorly printed picture fast shading into black and Aunt Avelina blending into the honeysuckle, her figure barely visible. Yes, she resembles my aunt, but look there. That's not her, the face is a smudge, practically black, you can't honestly say who it is. Looks like her, I can't deny that. There's a family resemblance, but this is Cousin Cloti, who was an Aunt Avelina lookalike. Matter of fact, you can't tell for sure who it is when a picture's blurred. Fact is, she's behind the honeysuckle. Yes, she was Cachimba's girlfriend, but she married someone else. She never loved him. She didn't like his name or share his ideas. We've never had anything to do with Cachimba – anything. We knew him, of course, the way everybody else in Hualacato knew him. That's the point, that's what you should keep in mind. In Hualacato we all know each other. But we're not to blame if she's Cachimba's wife. That's her business. We can be Avelina's friends or relatives, but not Cachimba's. She introduced him to me once, but I never laid eyes on him again. Hello, pleased to meet you, that was it. She gave us her photo because we're relatives, not because she's his wife. It was taken long before she met him. Besides, we haven't been on speaking terms with her for years. For that very reason – because we were against her marrying him. I was just telling you, I was just about to say in a letter I was trying to write to you, the pieces must be around here somewhere. It wasn't coming out right, my handwriting's not very good, I've got red spots on my back. I sometimes wonder if Cachimba ever existed or was someone Avelina made up. Please, couldn't we open the window a little just to let some air in?

Nabu goes on reading letters or poring over photographs. Who knows what may happen when he comes to a snap of Aunt Avelina. Perhaps nothing. We have so many aunts he may not even notice. Besides, he had the letter folder in his hands. I saw it plain as day. Tonight at least he won't get as far as the pictures. He'll be a good two days on the letters Roque wrote to me. It won't be pleasant if they start looking for Aunt Avelina as well. They'll plaster her picture everywhere. At the post office, just about to lick a stamp, someone'll lift his glance and see her poster, front and profile. Dogs sniffing her, she'll try to hide her eyes and cover her face to pass unnoticed. The guilty Avelina discovered at a party; send in the best dogs. The posters in the trains and buses showing the raw scar of a bite on her cheek, murderess, traitor, baby-killer, charged with putting razor blades in children's sledges. See for yourselves the number of boys and girls who cut themselves through no fault of their own while she went into hiding, laughing and mocking, half-concealed behind a honeysuckle bush in a snapshot inside a tin box. Light a fire and we'll burn the witch. This rat's unworthy of living among humankind. Just look at her red back. Of course, one of the posters will be sent here. He unrolls it, stares at it. But this is Aunt Avelina, Nabu will say.

Packs of hounds pad about in Kico's head. I just don't know, I can't remember, but when that honeysuckle snap was taken Cachimba was around. Singing or playing the guitar. It's a miracle he wasn't in the picture. But he might be in another. What if a picture of Cachimba turns up? Packs of black dogs sniffing after him in every nook and cranny of Hualacato. They clamp their jaws on an imagined Cachimba. They'll burst in here, rummage among our clothes in search of a shirt to sniff, tugging at the sleeves and collar, each after a scrap with Cachimba's scent. One of the dogs comes upon the tin box, he's just found Cachimba, he tosses him about with all the other photographs, the snapshots of the kids, they swarm in on Aunt Francisquita's wedding party just as the cake is about to be cut, knocking over wine glasses, ripping at the bodice of Auntie's white dress, tearing it off her, stripping her naked. Her back's red, fat, ugly. Aunt Francisquita's an old woman, her white dress is in shreds under the tables and chairs, the dogs are fighting over it. The lights go out. There in the midst of the throng is Cachimba. Auntie runs naked through the patios, clumsily, unable to escape. She falls. Seeing the spot on her back, and since she smells like Cachimba, the dogs set out in pursuit of her.

Leaping from one head to the next, the dogs reach Cholo. They are under his bed, looking for Avelina; later she'll lead them to Cachimba's cave, where Nabu will crush him underfoot like a lowly cockroach. Maddened, the dogs will crush the box, a slobbering fang will skewer the snapshots. Communions, weddings, stag nights, all the minor events of their lives hanging from one fang. The photos of Tite chewed and torn, he'll die all over again. The dogs delivering Avelina's picture to Nabu. And Nabu will say, look what you've made your family into – a bunch of criminals. You've hidden in your home the guiltiest of the guilty. You're all guilty. Wild horses will tear you limb from limb, as they did Tupac Amaru. Hurry, bring on the horses and ropes; there isn't a moment to lose. Nabu studying the photograph and dashing to his radios and telephones. Yes, I've hit on something big. Cholo and his wife were hiding the guilty party under their bed. They're all guilty, of course, nobody is innocent here. It's only a matter of getting them to talk. Yes, send the dogs. Unseen, Avelina scouring the house for a place to hide Cachimba's shirt so that the dogs won't find it. As if she were already dead, she flutters about the rooms, an invisible bug breathing. Black-winged Uvelina flapping in a corner, a funereal bird with no escape. Nabu has found her, he's switched on all the lights, shuts the doors and windows, there isn't a single cranny where she can hide. Nocturnal Avelina is cornered, with rags in her beak. Cachimba's clothes are hidden at the Aballays', you can send that, look what you've made your family into, you've lost your father, children, a wife who loved you. It's all your fault, hello, hello, come in, over, we're holding Cachimba's chief accomplices, and foremost among them of course is Cholo, alias Cholo. He has a great red blotch on his back and conspicuous distinguishing marks. Every-one's implicated, but he's at the heart of it, he's destroyed his own family, there's never been a crime like it. Yes, but don't forget we have no photographs of Cachimba. Just a snapshot of his wife cutting honeysuckle blossoms; it was at her hen party, please take that into consideration. It was a get-together of friends and relatives. I imagine Cachimba was up to the same with his own relatives, that's what stag nights and hen parties are like. They aren't for the couple, each half celebrates on his or her own, otherwise it's no fun. Anyway, Avelina's only a cousin of ours. Calling her aunt is an old family habit, that's all. Not even a close cousin, which is why Cachimba means nothing to us. He's an in-law at best, and that isn't blood. Same as Cousin Roque. Nobody knows him but we have his photo at home. As you can see, we're all innocent. There might be a picture of Cachimba, but that wouldn't change our innocence. He may have arrived unnoticed towards the end of the party, otherwise they would have pulled his leg, because the custom is to stay away from the fiancée on what is her last day as a free woman. He probably kept to one side, playing his guitar and singing something. Maybe he drank a glass of wine and left, perhaps his photo got taken too, you can't tell, but he only came at the end of the party to see his fiancée home. By then it was quite dark. We're respectable people, ask anybody. We believe in the Virgin; you'll find lots of little photos of her in some of the other boxes. We're all baptised, we're all God's children, just like you people. We don't kill or steal, we just do our weaving. That's how we make a living, though we did own land in the past. It was taken from us, but we never caused any trouble over it. You must believe me, we're decent people, we have our memories, good and bad ones, we've gone through our share of suffering – when Tite died, for instance. Do you think for a minute we'd have been up to anything with our Tite dead? OK, I don't deny that on that one occasion we kept silent. I stopped my machine at the factory, and here at home the loom was stopped, though it hardly makes any noise. But almost all of Hualacato did the same. You people had just arrived, you were making a lot of noise, our eardrums were splitting. So we went silent – just to find out who was banging the drums. You could hear them everywhere, you know that. You didn't want us to hear, you didn't want to stand out. Why bang the drums then? But that was all. We went back to work, poor as ever, just to keep body and soul together; the rest end up far away from here. To pay for other things, we do a bit of extra weaving overtime at home and even so the kids go barefoot, we're short of milk, bread, meat, basic health care, there's diarrhoea in the summer, the kids get dehydrated, they go limp as punctured balloons. In Hualacato there's a limbo full of little angels who see no light and get no milk, that's right, we heard it when we stopped all noise that day, we heard it clearly with the drums. I didn't make any noise that day because I wanted to find out why Tite had died. One has a right, I am, was, his father. Are they going to deny us that as well? We can't even talk about it. It's forbidden. When someone brings it up, you people wag a finger at him. Cachimba, you shout. Careful, they're all Cachimbas. And you go after him with your dogs, the dogs go after the Cachimbas while you watch over our poverty. Look, I'm not worried about myself, not after Tite and all this. Unleash your dogs, if you want. Anybody here can be Cachimba, especially if he has a photo of Avelina in a tin box. If you'd guarantee my family could go free, I'd be willing to say, see here, I'm Cachimba, stop looking for him. And that'd be the end of it. They would lead me away and get on to something else. Why run the risk of taking the picture that's in your folder? They'll cart me to the accident ward and put me in a big bed. The nurses will shake their heads from side to side. An endemic disease, they'll say, sorry, it's impossible, there's no cotton wool. Look at the cartons, all empty, we can't remove the spots

from your back, a timely rain would have solved everything, but you can tell how hot this summer's been, say
the nurses, seeing there's no more cotton. If you already
have Cachimba, what do you need a photo of Avelina for?
It's ridiculous. So let them sleep in peace, let Coca breathe
normally, there's no longer any danger. Let Sila and Kico
stop worrying, neither of them can be Cachimba, one
Cachimba should be enough. And Nabu can relax. Thanks
to him, they'll say, and they'll pin medals on him, a trip to
Europe, all expenses paid. On the high seas Nabu will tell
people how he tracked down Cachimba. It was thanks to
this, he'll say, opening a folder and showing the snapshot
of Avelina by the honeysuckle. No, don't show it, it's too
much for us, it must be horrible, other travellers will say.
A real monster, Nabu will say, closing his folder, a monster
with a red blotch across her back, a real clot on Avelina's
back. What's more, she used to put razor blades in the
little children's sledges. Please, we don't want to hear such
dreadful things, it's too awful, the travellers will say, taken
aback. And the sea breeze on Nabu's face, his shirt
ballooning in profile against the waves, as he sips a soft
drink, his gaze on the horizon.

The old man hears Belinda's footfall – a staccato, nervous
trot from one shelf to the next, a series of great leaps over
the furniture. Punctuated by long pauses, in which she is
obviously watching or looking for something, her tail
twitching. Then another little trot across a piece of furniture and the sound of her paws on the floor. Suddenly her
claws scratching at the back of a chair or a crate of bottles.
Next to the hat boxes, bolting from all those present. Ugly
pong in the house tonight, Belinda probably thinks to
herself, ugly the flood of perspiration in all these bodies,
ugly the smell of the begonias, ugly the way that big spoon
hangs in the kitchen, the pot on the wall, ugly too the

percussionist's brightly lit room, the glass wall. He's shuffling papers, making a phone call, polishing his baton as he reads old letters or studies photographs. The old man reconstructs all this from the cat's nervous toing and froing, he sees that even she is aware of Avelina's presence drifting through the house. If we could just talk, agree on what to say when questioned in turn about the photo. Agree, think of something to say, the kids found it in the street, they liked the honeysuckle, as simple as that. Or say, all right, we know her but we never met Cachimba. Whatever we say, he won't care. We can't tell him anything, just as we can't ask him for anything. He's here to question people, not to listen to them. Nothing we say is any good as long as Avelina's picture is here. A picture's worth a thousand words. The fact is that Avelina's a relative of ours only by chance. A relative? No more than a relative? That alone will do it, all of us will be taken to the south, to the pits, to the rivers. Or else he'll say, look, I don't care whether you are this woman's relatives or not. The only thing that matters to me is that you are in possession of her photograph. You knew full well the risk you were running keeping such a document here. Why say anything, then? There's nothing to say. You've brought all this on yourselves. You're nothing but Cachimba's accomplices. Nobody can save you now, not even me. This is what I came for. Now it's all over. Tomorrow you'll be transferred to suitable units. Nothing will be left of this house, not even the cat, you can rest assured of that. And off they will all go down a dirt road in a lorry, he in the middle, his chair bouncing about, Hualacato there in the distance, that's where we were born and we'll never see it again, the lorry jolting over stony ground. Look, Sila will say from one side of the vehicle. And there'll be the house going up in smoke, not a trace of the Aballays left. With everything burning, the red-hot weathercock begins to buckle in the heart of the flames.

I've got to make up something, the old man was telling himself, when he hears Belinda's thump at the door and he sees her come in through the transom window. Her bow is twisted. Has she caught it against something or is it just her nerves? She leaps to the old man's side, purring, rubbing her head against him, all perfectly normal, but her heart is fluttering, upset by something she does not yet know. Avelina. How can he transmit it, the old man wonders, and he begins to tap the nearby walls, first of Cholo and Coca's room, then of Kico's. Languages are born on their own, out of extreme necessity. When a thing has to be named, the first sound uttered fits it, and there you have your word. Things become real in the search for a word for them. Old Aballay's *tapping* stems from a single fact and can mean only one thing, the snapshot of Avelina, already foretold by Belinda's paws tripping over the furniture. Cholo and Coca get the message on one side, as does Kico on the other, but not Sila and the kids, away on the far side of one of the percussionist's rooms. The others reply by tapping, the first thing has been named, we have the first word of the language. Mother. Now it's easy to add something about the object mentioned; one tap more, a slight change in its intensity, and there it is, because only one thing can be said about Avelina's photo, one possible thing. Get it out of the box. And the word leaps up, virginal, with all its synonyms. The only way to remove the red spots, so that each of them will get air, is to move the begonia pots into the light, where they will turn green again. All this by a few taps on the wall. From here on it will be a matter of adding rhythms, spoons on the tabletop, feet on the floor, or something quieter, like eyes and fingertips. To talk in his presence without his being aware of it. To speak about Aunt Avelina right under his nose. And with each invented word they will have something new, with the right word they may someday even manage to drive Nabu out of the house. Filled with happy dreams, the old man's brain bubbles over as he strokes Belinda's back, his head teeming with as yet unfamiliar words.

The percussionist had dozed off reading Roque's letters, miniscule handwriting, the same phrases repeated, reading the pages without understanding a thing, eyes running automatically over the words without an idea as to what they meant. Boring letters but they had to be read, for at any moment they might reveal a clue, some hint or careless expression, a word to clear everything up. He was at the bottom of the warren, the least little hair could prove important in trapping his quarry. At any moment all Roque's nonsense might turn on its head and yield some meaning. Expressions like 'I'm only led by good intentions' and 'your words allow me a ray of hope' become cryptic signals. He reluctantly picked up his torch for the nightly inspection round before turning in, opened the French door, and smelled the pong, their presence. Stale sweat? Hot damp earth? Unspeakable odours coming in through the transoms. There's usually dry dung at the bottom of a warren, a smell of dry dirt in the claws, heavy breath, the old smell of prisons. No, not that either. The smell of a cat in labour? Cat sperm? A cat on heat? More a noise than an odour, but inaudible, a blowing added to the silence. As if as one the Aballays were shouting from within, smelling from within. Nabu unsealed the old man's door and turned the light on him. The old man was deep into something, forging a language made up of but two words, and he was confronted with the urgent necessity to invent a word for Cachimba. It hovered about the house, all he had to do was give it a sound to make it go away.

Avelina's ghost had been laid the moment they found a word for it. Old fish, a freshly dug root? Stale sweat? The torch lit up the old man's submissive face, Nabu's foot spun the old man's body round in the beam of light. The red spots on Aballay's back reminded Nabu of those features that distinguish a species, the fox's tail, the bird's bill, no, the pong was coming from somewhere else.

When Cholo saw the percussionist's face behind the light he wanted to say something but his voice went dead. No breath reached his vocal chords, all his strength was concentrated in his hands, which clutched his chest. They weren't going to take that away from him without a fight.

'Your fears are a nuisance.' Nabu's words came to him clearly through the light of the torch. 'Pretend you're not afraid and maybe we can have some peace and all get a good night's sleep. This house stinks of your fear. Take this pill and go to sleep at once.'

Cholo stuck one hand out from his chest, just one, and received the pill.

'You're afraid too,' Nabu said to Coca. He sounded like a doctor.

'Yes, a little,' said Coca, her voice extending out from her.

'Take this pill. I've already told you two I'm not here to destroy but to save you. Your fear stems from bad thoughts. From what you know but keep bottled up.'

He went through the house shining his light into corners and up into the ceilings. When he was satisfied that nothing visible was producing that blend of smell and sound, he threw open a window to let the fear out.

5

HOUSE ARREST WAS turning the place into a big vat for dyeing clothes. And the vat was filled with a solution of bleach in preparation for a white mourning. As they stirred and stirred, the Aballays found that they too were fading, and they began to look at each other as if they were figures in over-developed photographs, as if they were somebody else. Like the time Aunt Avelina got back from her honeymoon by the sea. What a tan she had, what a perfect complexion! Yes, but look at her shoulders. Once she had pulled down her dress straps, Aunt Avelina's tanned shoulders were like watermelons in the sun. The Aballays were the same, only the other way round. How pale, how white they were. The old man's wrinkles were white stripes; Coca and Cholo were chalk-stained and were hybridising under the effect of chemicals that changed their skin colour and made them look like something kept all its life in a cellar. The dyes were turning the Aballays' skins almost as pale as Nabu's. The family, having turned from a shade of night to fake white, no longer looked as if it hailed from Hualacato. Whitest of all was Julito, sucking his dummy in his cradle all day and looking like a frozen fish. Snaps retouched by Bocha. How does Grandad come out so white? Lab tricks, laughed Bocha, done in the printing. We can get a nice white skin quite unlike the original.

The rain — what was it, what will it be like? A real marvel. Something almost without name, for it creates its own sound, is its own word. Rain must be seen, the rest it does by itself. In winter, rain was fritters and photographs. In summer, a real feast, and we called it a thunderstorm. A year without rain, and then a downpour. The rain falling on the hills came to Hualacato like a floodtide. The streets turned into rivers smelling of grass, and everybody went out in it, sloshing their feet in it and letting the rain come down on them. Every street a river, from north to south one river running next to another, roaring rivers that carried away microbes and endemic diseases. Goats fattened, milk was plentiful, grass sprouted, the deadly vinchucas drowned, and when the sun came out again everything was washed clean.

For the kids, these things were stories told by their grandfather. Of the rains, they only knew thunder. They heard it from their rooms, changing colour and staring at the walls. They stared as if they wanted to return to a place they were unsure of. With blanched hands and etiolated feet, they stared at the walls, the tiny holes, a stain in the plaster, brush marks, cracks in the lime wash, places where at any moment the little spider might dash out in a fright, white places that had no birthdays and waited for the little spider. Whoever first spotted it wins a prize, a big lump of sugar.

An ordinary torch is always handy for checking the time. Comes the sound of seals being broken, then the torchlight counting heads, heralding the dawn. Let's see, one, two, three, everyone's there, the light goes out. Nabu moves on to open other doors, for day is breaking, sunrise is at hand.

And another day dawns amid bells and whistles, the etiolated little birds hovering over posters that stand for walls that do not exist but that are respected. They are out of bounds. Breakfast in silence while Nabu reads out what they will do that day. It's a day for weaving and making paper birds, and there will be an interesting sermon. The old man can draw if he likes, as the birds he cuts out are quite ugly. By the end of the year there will be an exhibition of them, and this unit must win first prize. They must cut out toads, finches, swallows, hippos, sailing boats, and elephants. Try a sea-horse, which is very hard. Chinese fish are highly rated in competitions. There's also the llama, whale, and swan. After that you may try your hand at deer and penguins, both intricate. Later on, the heron and the crab. And after supper, story-telling. Tonight's the old man's turn. I'm going to pay close attention. Tonight he'll tell me about his compadre and his mysterious postcards. So start thinking about your answers, don't forget anything, and you've got the whole day to recall things about the compadre. And now each of you back to your place, no, not that way, don't forget there's a wall there.

Could anyone have imagined that Aunt Avelina would turn out to be so important? She had been little more than a snapshot that you skipped over or gave a quick glance. Aunt Avelina was something you gradually overlooked, like Roque. Ah, Roque, how could I ever forget him? That's a lie, Roque's entirely forgettable. If it weren't for his picture, the name Roque would have slipped out of memory. It was almost the same with Aunt Avelina – a snapshot and a couple of seaside postcards. Still, how clear it all looks now. Her white face, the embroidered flowers round the hem of her dress, the way she laughed, the way she draped herself on Cachimba's arm, suddenly so real, her 'today we have to keep quiet, not say a word, stop weaving, stop laughing, stop talking, because they're here and if we keep quiet maybe we'll find out what they're doing in Hualacato and, even better, others may find out'. Her 'some day things will change but you can't just stand around waiting for it to happen'. Her 'don't buy what they sell, no matter how good it looks, because it's all rubbish'. Her 'what a party we'll have the day they leave'. Her 'let's postpone our joy till then'. Her 'take these books, don't miss a chance; at least you can read, when over half Hualacato can't. All they know how to read is their machines in the shop and their ploughs in the field'. How beautiful what she said then, before the dogs bit her and her shoulders were like ripe watermelons when she got back from the sea. How different she looks now. Like the difference between the snapshot with the honeysuckle and the photo pinned up in every post office and railway station, in every village no matter how small, posters of Avelina the baby-killer. The dogs know her face by heart, front and side views, as the trains pull out, tacked beside a poster for a horror film opening next week.

They talk as they weave, like tapping your feet in time to music. The sun isn't up yet but they are already at their looms, practising their own language and reviewing the two phrases they know, *Avelina's photo* and *take it out of the box*. The first to move will try the word *when*, that's it, little words that form themselves, with the answer treading on their heels, shaped by the blink of an eye, you know what *when cats yowl and he goes out* means. The old man shows off the word *who*, lowering his eyebrows, and Kico makes up the word *I* with a fleeting gesture. The old man writes everything down in a notebook, each word a little drawing. A beautiful alphabet of signs that are taps, winks, finger figures, coughs, and throat clearings, as well

47

as little songs. And their notes. With such a song, Coca makes up the word *no*, which also means *it's very dangerous, I'm against it, I don't want to*, with expressive equivalents in her eyes, which open wider than they should in a pale face that has nothing to do with house arrest, as her hands fall quiet over her work. But all languages have ugly words, blame it on things, not on the languages. It would never have occurred to anyone to make up the word *death* if the thing called death did not exist. Two hands knitting, but without needles, means *death*. All of them understand, especially Kico, who at once makes up its opposite by crossing two fingers and showing them to everybody, and nobody objects to its obvious meaning, *life*, which the old man draws in his notebook with a gesture meaning *nice word*, and so the word *word* now has its word, associated with *nice*, to boot, which at the same time seems to mean *making up a language can be great fun*. The sign meaning *life* has its synonym in big bold letters, *risk*, and then Cholo makes up *but how*. There are a number of suggestions of a hesitant nature that nobody understands and this the old man sums up in a drawing that means *doubt*. Then, out of a swaying movement, comes the word *door*, together with its most obvious synonyms, *seals*, *bars*, *difficult*, and *impossible*, and remembering the opening through which Belinda comes in and out, the old man makes a gesture (which he writes down without asking) that means *transom window*. And they all see Kico climbing up the door, one foot on the latch, and slipping through the transom in search of Aunt Avelina's photo. Coca starts a word meaning *tears*, *goodbye*, *good luck*, *have a nice trip*, and Cholo another that means *careful, son, it's too difficult but that's life* – all pure sentimentality. Coca agrees, and with a tap and cracking sound she utters for the first time words for *there's no going back*, *farewell*, *waving handkerchiefs*, *we'll be waiting for you*, *take care*, and *how we love you, my dear*. And, coolly, Kico seems to be saying, *OK, cut the crap, tomorrow you'll find Aunt Avelina's picture gone and all our fears as well*. The old man hasn't hands enough to draw so many words, he forgets about his arthritis, arthrosis, and other words of that ilk and looks like a violinist giving a good performance of a very difficult passage. In the end he picks up a stack of paper, making up the word *dictionary*, which also means a *pause*, or *stop talking for a bit*. The dictionary seems unnecessary now that the language is unfolding all on its own. That's what they all say, anyway, even though after a pause the old man goes on with his drawings. Just what you'd expect of an old man, after all. We must overlook his peevishness, such postures at his time of life are sometimes respectable.

It's awful to eat without speaking. Sucking up soup and the sound of spoons against teeth are quite disagreeable. Like new-born kittens clumsily lapping milk from the same bowl. The kids have not yet learned to hold a spoon according to the new regulations. It clatters against the edge of their plates, spilling soup or scattering mashed potatoes. How disagreeable it is to hear them chewing and swallowing all at the same time, to hear jaws working in their sad, stupid way. A spoon scraping the bottom of the plate when the soup is nearly finished is insufferable – to say nothing of the noise our mouths make. You're like a pig at a trough. The old man, lacking teeth, makes awful sounds with his gums and tongue. Why, when he always ends up whisking his food around a couple of times and then swallows it whole? Before Nabu, words covered up such excesses. Now, however, each of us is a clumsy little animal. Don't slurp your soup, you have to stick your spoon into it and then swallow, however hot it is. To slurp it from your spoon is rude, the noise unpleasant. If everyone sucked up their soup, meals would be a torment. Just imagine a noise like that added to difficult breathing. To eat soup properly the nose has to be quite clean. Pigs, Nabu must be thinking. It's obvious that eating noises make him edgy. For a change, and also to avoid unpleasant sounds, they decide their spoons are pencils, and to the rhythm of the former implement their dictionary keeps growing, while Nabu wanders about looking at his watches. The meal becomes a boring rhythm of spoons alone, knives and forks having been absolutely forbidden. But food like this requires no other tool, nor does their language. They eat and are blanched, and as they blanch they become wormy. They are tiny silkworms eating mulberry leaves in a shoe box. Little worms mastering their own language. The Aballays don't miss a linguistic chance, they are like an ant's feelers, the movements of a bee, spoons rising to sketch ideograms in the air. There is almost nothing they cannot say now. There are only two possible causes for fear tonight: Kico popping back in through the transom and the old man being questioned, for today's his turn. But the old man makes them relax, telling them his compadre's not Cachimba but his fiftyish work mate the coffee man, who sends postcards for the fun of it. The man does everything as if he were playing. The meal has also been a farewell to Kico, a kind of stag party, for popping out through the transom is like getting married. Lots of luck in your new life. Cholo feels he's growing old and will become a grandfather should Kico get married. But Cholo doesn't like the bride; he'd never have dreamed that Kico would be marrying Aunt Avelina, still less her photograph.

Eventually Nabu's sermons become like the sound of a wordless meal – chewing and more chewing and the unpleasant din of a spoon scraping the bottom of a plate. They sit on the stomach like lead. Fat is hard to digest while listening to the same old story, boring sermons about boring life, the boring population explosion in Latin America, and other similar topics.

'Today I'm going to talk about the importance of paper cut-outs in the modern world' – here Nabu's spoons clash – 'which will come as news to you here in Hualacato. This activity, or science really, has been introduced into this town as therapy for impatience. When you're impatient all sorts of nonsense goes through your heads, and these are the cause of all your misfortune. I won't put up with grimaces or bored looks. Open your eyes and clear your minds. Especially you children. The rest are hopeless. It's you children who have to take this in for the future. Listen carefully, for I'm going to ask you to repeat all I've said. Don't forget, I've got a box full of scorpions, spiders, basilisks, and snakes.'

A quick spoon movement by Sila launched the nascent language's first insult. One of those insults that covers any offence and that fills the mouth, lingering on the teeth and tongue and caressing the palate as the invective pours out, leaving you as unruffled as a stagnant puddle. For a first-rate insult the mouth cavity is not enough. The whole head must become a sound box, and the mouth a channel for compressed air. Then the insult will emerge like a shot, and even after it's out will leave a satisfying aftertaste, a peace that will restore your harmony with the world. Sila's aftertaste made the round of everyone's mouth, and they all nodded their heads in satisfaction. Even Nabu found Sila's insult intelligible, and while his words never faltered he shot her a blank look. The family's satisfaction was understandable. It was the first time they had been able to insult Nabu. The old man made a mental note of the insult so as to be able to sketch it later on. It was quite a discovery, a real monument of language.

'Apparently,' read Nabu aloud, 'the symbols I taught you for cutting out paper birds mean "fold back", "fold and turn back to dot", and "permanent fold". It's not a question of learning the technique parrot-fashion. All this, as I've said, has a clear, exact meaning, which is to teach you patience. Paper cut-outs are not, as you may suppose, a modern invention. They go back to the year 100. Times were hard; paper birds appeared in China to fulfil a great need. One of the founders of this science is none other than Boadjair Dharma, the inventor of karate. From China, such birds reached Japan, where the art has been practised down to this day. I will show you the admirable creations of the great Akira Hoshizawa. Unfortunately, paper birds took hundreds of years to reach our language area, for it was only at the end of the twelfth century that the Moors introduced paper into Spain, and, along with it, paper cut-outs. Centuries later, luminaries like Unamuno, Pérez de Ayala, and Jacinto Benavente took up the calling, and eventually, in Spain, in 1938, Dr Vicente Solorzano Sagredo wrote his famous treatise on the subject in ten or twelve tomes. In its foreword, he holds that bird cut-outs might well be the new way to train the minds that will build improved civilisations.'

The children had begun to blink fast when Nabu suddenly launched into his final paragraph, in which he chewed over the strange list of paper-bird geniuses, his tongue galloping between his teeth, the names ringing out like the sound of a spoon scraping an empty plate.

'Do you know who Kashara, Neal Elías, Robert Harbin, Edward Kallop, Shizuko Moshizuki, and John Andreas are?' he hammered on. 'All paper-bird experts. Now then, you must regard each new bird you cut out as one more weird notion cut out of your head. Let's see if we can't once and for all cleanse you of nonsense so that you can look at life as it really is and drop all this idiocy, which only leads to ruin. May you profit from this lesson, and now back to your places of work without any comment whatsoever.'

It would be different with a pair of scissors, but of course they're forbidden. You fold the paper, pressing the fold down hard and running your nail over it so as to be able to cut it evenly, but you can't concentrate – not with the old man in there for an hour. With scissors you could just cut away and that would be it. When you fold the paper with your nail, sometimes it cuts neatly but other times the edges come out ragged, with useless little tears, and in the end the paper bird looks awful. The worst thing of all is when, after running your nail along the crease so many times, you cut the paper and it still tears. Folding the paper and running your tongue over the dampened fold so as to be able to cut it neatly doesn't work either as there are always ragged edges sticking out and you end up with a burning tongue. Well, this is what being patient means. I wonder how the old man's getting on in his exam? The questions are hard, and things never go smoothly. Get me the old man, Nabu said, and the old man took himself off on his own, perfectly calm. Don't worry, he said, I know the subject inside out, I know everything about the compadre almost by heart. Get me the old man, the same as you say get me a pair of socks. He must be running him through the verbs. What a way to end the day. Relax, the old man said with brand-new words as he was leaving, if it's about postcards I know the subject cold. Well, he was always the optimist, but they were sending him to hospital for an emergency operation, room four, bed ninety-five, here's your nightshirt, your bedpan, here's the chart that

53

marks your temperature. We still have to study your tests and X-rays. Doctors can often convey everything with a look or a nod of the head and anyway there's never any cotton wool in these hospitals. The ships bringing it always sink. The worst is having to wait outside when the patient is in the operating room. There are always nurses dashing in and out, you never know why, until suddenly the doctor appears, a look on his face as if he is going to give you bad news, but no, he only came out to consult briefly with some colleague or to see to one of those medical inspectors who keep pestering him, in which case everything seems to be going well. But you have a nagging doubt and you shyly approach him. Well, doctor? one says in these cases, expecting the worst, but the doctor has a serene face, and when you ask about the patient he screws up his brow, lost in thought. Ah, he says at last, you mean the sick man. We've operated, he's resting in his room, out of danger. And all the while you'd been devouring cigarettes and your fingernails, your mind racing with foolish ideas. In cases of this kind, you are better off cutting out paper birds.

Trouble is, the old man was never much good at verb tenses. He grew up in a rural area among people who had no white blood and spoke the original tongue of Hualacato. Talk to him about horses or birds or trapping cougars or condors – that's his line. But forget verbs. He doesn't know a thing about postcards either. He's a transplant, he's always trying to adapt. But he feels the call of the woods, the open air, the world of his ancestors, their tales, witchcraft. He says the word in a mocking way, but he loves it. On this side of things, he does his best with verbs. To be on this side you have to know how to conjugate them, especially during an operation, when conjugating verbs is like breathing and is absolutely vital to the patient.

A pair of good lungs always helps you out of danger. Learning to read at the age of fifty was too much for him ever to get caught up in history. Lost in the complexities of European monarchies, he never got past feudalism. All of it struck him as unreal, made up just to fill books. Reality for the time being was something beyond his reach. His missing leg, for instance. Something of the sort. At night he complained about the pain in his leg. Anything wrong? Yes, my leg's hurting. Here, rub it with this, it'll do you good. And he'd laugh. No, it's my missing leg that hurts.

The old man left the percussionist's room under his own steam, propelling his wheelchair with one hand. He went straight to his room, contravening no regulations, full of dignity. It was hard to tell whether he was white or pale, but in neither case was it because of house arrest. He had the impassive face of a person coming out of an exam; you had no idea how he had done. See him to his room, he's a bit tired, said Nabu's voice. When Sila took over the wheelchair, the old man's hand let go of the wheel and dangled there. He sat nearly upright in the chair and it was also a stretcher down an imaginary corridor between posters, a long hospital corridor. Covered with a white sheet but alive, he was going to bed to rest after the long day. Everything's fine, he said, using a new word. That is, Nabu still knew nothing about Avelina, otherwise things would have been different. Obviously Nabu had not yet examined the photographs, involved as he was with Roque's postcards and letters. In an atmosphere of anaesthesia bottles and oxygen tubes, the old man went to his room. He had managed to conjugate every verb, but he was exhausted. It was like a sunset. At last the long day drew to a close. Everything written and read by Nabu that morning was finally over. What with paper birds, sermons, and questioning, all that seemed a long time ago.

Everyone to bed now. Waiting for cats to yowl and Nabu to go out with his stock of flares and hand grenades. If only the cats wailed louder than ever tonight. There were lots of cats on the walls and rooftops, and the trees were full of them. For Nabu. Ten minutes, ten precious minutes of cats and cries, then Nabu would come out into the patio and Kico could slip through the transom. The whole wall was lined with cats, all their ears cocked.

But there are no cats or ears anywhere, just a shameless moon glinting in the broken glass on the walls. Weather vane catless too, nobody knows where Belinda is, and Kico waiting for the caterwauling. Any moment now and it will begin. There's a light wind; as soon as it blows over the cats will start in. The breeze passes but after a while it returns to blow papers down the streets, raise dust, and whistle through the weathercock and the bits of broken glass. Dust drifts in doorways, the wind sniffs its way inside, until the beam of Nabu's fluttering torch comes along. Let's see, he counts, one, two, three. And, as everyone knows, no sooner has the torch passed than it begins to grow light.

6

AS IF FLEEING FROM something, Nabu came at the double, looking as though he'd heard a pack of cats, and he made the Aballays stand against the wall exactly as they had on the first day. That's it, up against the wall with your eyes searching for a little spider. Keep your mouths shut and don't move a muscle. As he frisked them he spoke in a swallowing sort of way, while they gulped down their own saliva. He had not come from his room, from studying photographs, as they had feared. He came from theirs, where he'd been carrying out a routine inspection, rummaging amongst their clothes and mattresses, once again turning out the contents of wardrobes, emptying drawers on to the floor, buttons scattering under the bed, garments thrown over a shelf, the kids' picture cards under the furniture. Against the wall like the first time. Minutes flew by, vanishing in seconds; in a nervous, headlong rush from their quarters to the room where they worked at their weaving, the percussionist robbed them of elapsed time, disorientating them yet again. No longer was the worst part having to put up with the situation – it was trying to understand Nabu's logic. In spite of the ban on talking, the Aballays could easily have communicated by means of their hands or feet, but they were so completely adrift now that no form of language made any difference.

The percussionist never shouted. Speaking in a moderately loud voice, he gave all words the same value. It was a kind of drone that spared him both loudness and silence. His manner derived from neither the words he chose nor the emphasis he placed on them; his aesthetic, his style, lay in his ferocity. But this time he was shouting, which threw them even more, for now, as well as not grasping his logic, they did not even know who Nabu was. Something was happening to him. Perhaps he'd had a reminder from his superiors, forbidding him something as well. Or a letter preparing him for bad news. Maybe he had been saving his shouts for an extremely grave situation, and this was it. The imaginary spider that was taking shape, or Aunt Avelina, within range of each pair of eyes, crawling up the wall on eight legs. Or Cachimba. The shout distorted Nabu's words, especially his final syllables, which came across in a confusing falsetto. In raising his voice he made it impossible for them to believe a word he uttered, shouting stripped him of all power of conviction, and what he said was utter nonsense. He was like the little drunk who once mistakenly found his way into their house. Nabu's shouts were like a round-up of unconnected words looking for harmonious agreement, an orchestra tuning up, each musician trying out a different bit. *Incredible*, *damage*, *betrayed trust*, *spoon* – the words went round and round without managing to say anything. *Spoon* seemed to be the one reiterated element; Nabu was shouting it as if he were crying fire or something equally desperate. But *spoon* was the word that eventually calmed them, for the worst they could have heard just then was the word *photograph*, and every clue showed that Nabu was still far afield. After ten minutes of further lost words and dropped syllables, they began putting together some of the pieces of the puzzle. The reason for Nabu's anger was a spoon he found in one of the rooms during his tour of inspection. A spoon of all things, as if it were a conflagration or natural catastrophe. They knew they were not allowed to take any objects other than wooden ones to their rooms. But it was only a spoon, and it was hard to grasp what ultimate meaning he was trying to give the word above and beyond his voice and shout. A spoon, so sorry a shape, and amongst other objects so humble and limited in use. A spoon meant only eating soup or taking cough medicine – in the logic of Hualacato, at least. In Nabu's logic, however, the spoon, spinning round in his mind, ended up making a victim of the percussionist. You knew taking things to your rooms is forbidden. But you think I'm made of iron. I've been locked up here as long as the rest of you, the only difference is that I've been lonely (which came across to them as loony). The previous Nabu seemed distant. This, the true one, was suddenly revealed. Not only had he managed to turn a spoon into something else but he himself was now something else.

'Anything wrong?' asked one of the kids between clenched teeth.

'No, nothing, our little drunkard's just gone off his rocker. He'll get over it.'

Have you forgotten this is a war? Nabu was saying behind their backs. A war? The Aballays wondered where the other side was. Spoons, wars, tiny spiders – Nabu must be stinking drunk. It was hard to understand how with a few simple shouts he had magically turned a spoon into a fire, a house into a war. A magician plucking three doves out of an empty top hat is no trick, since the birds actually fly across the room.

Nothing was left of the spoon, not even the word. Its

old meaning gone, no longer attached to soup and cough medicine, the spoon was dead. As the spoon expired, Nabu became more animated and quickly began to take a definitive shape. A stronger, surer Nabu took the stage, real now, as the former Nabu faded into dream. Blending madness – the truest part of him, perhaps – into his nature, he gave things back their hidden meaning. Things, gaping wounds. Fate. He had somehow cleared the cobwebs out of their heads, and now it would be difficult to view the world anew. They had spent their lives celebrating birthdays, visiting relatives, and staring into photographs at people and objects they regarded as important. But that was not so. Being alive and living in Hualacato was something quite different. A wound. But not the kind cured in three or four days by some home remedy. Parties and snapshots were foolish. So much time wasted in silliness. Having sewn Aunt Francisquita's wedding dress. Having answered that fool Roque's letters. Letting the kids be born unaware that one day the percussionist and his ultimate truths would come marching through the door. Growing old to find out that spoons die too.

You can turn round, Nabu said, recovering his drone. He was smoothing his clothes and hair, as if he had just strode in from riding or hunting. It was impossible to fathom why he had spoken to them without letting them look at him. There was no reason for it. Maybe he was afraid they might discover the source of his power to turn spoons into fires. His drone, breaking up words for ever, was now worse than his shouts. He spoke and things changed as he looked at them; everything he named changed its meaning. If we're at war, he said in a way that was like an echo of his shouts, we aren't going to throw flowers at you. War, he was saying, and all of a sudden – created by his word – the enemy appeared, for you cannot have war without two opposing sides. By a magician's trick on the part of the percussionist, the Aballays were suddenly turned into the enemy army, and these wounds would not be cured by home remedies. He said war the way he said spoon, holding up the one he had found in the upstairs bedroom. But it was no longer a spoon. Stripped of everything else, the spoon was twisting in his hands like an old rag, living out its last few moments as a spoon, drifting off, passing like a noise in the night, saying its final goodbyes, falling distantly into the sea, a setting sun.

Go back to your rooms, Nabu told the enemy. They turned their heads all at the same time like little soldiers and made their way down a long corridor, spoonless, the old man in the vanguard, wheelchair creaking, the others behind, tallest first, and Belinda bringing up the rear. They marched down the new corridor, which was something else now, towards their rooms, which were something else, along what was clearly a passageway even if it had no supporting walls. Down this passageway the defeated enemy marched, counting their casualties, the words the percussionist had killed that day, an incredible number of words slain in a few minutes' time.

They trudged along, oblivious of where they were putting their feet, looking for something without knowing what. They had forgotten something vital but remembered its name. They came back empty handed, knowing they had been carrying whatever it was when they had been made to stare at the wall. Yes, we lost it on the way. What do we do now? What was it? I don't know, I had it in my hands – I'm sure of it. It must be somewhere around, I was carrying it, it was here in my hands. They did not have the word for it. They had no way of knowing that what had been lost was reality.

Shut up, the percussionist told them, as if they had any words left, unaware that they were burying them. On the enemy trudged in silence, somewhere between wars and corridors, turning to the language they were making up so as to preserve both words and life. Swallowing saliva so as to blot out all they had heard.

That night they had no supper (a punishment set out by the regulations; Nabu seldom improvised). From the sermon on the spoon they went straight into night, locked up in their rooms. Nabu switched off the lights earlier than usual, which was only logical. Now that they were no longer the Aballays but the enemy, some things had to change. They could hear the percussionist's low voice as he spoke over his radio. Metallic answers coming from God knows where, the telephone that seemed to have always belonged to him, the instrument of his secrets, the telephone over which Aunt Francisquita's voice had so often reached them in the past.

What came through, in fact, was Sila and the kids' voices singing in their room. On occasions like this Sila always made them sing, and sing away they did, reluctant and sleepily. Old songs of that locale, which helped them remember they still were in Hualacato. The song seemed to come from a long way off, its sound leaping from one transom to the next in Belinda's wake. The song broke off abruptly when they heard the bell calling for silence, be good and quiet, go to bed and stay there till morning without breaking the rules. From this moment on night-time regulations were in force, the book with blue covers that contained only prohibitions and punishments. A book to instil fear, read out in instalments during the course of sermons, full of unknown judges, invisible tribunals, and unmentionable zoos. A book rarely out of his hands, encased in see-through plastic so as to keep its delicate binding fresh. The bell, and *crick*, the cricket stops singing when it hears footsteps. The kids go silent.

From the kitchen comes the sound of singing forks. The spoon is very clumsy, too bulky, too heavy, with a dullish noise when it grazes a plate, and worse if it falls to the floor, an unreverberating *plop*. By contrast, the fork, with its shrillness, has a festive air. Clinking cheerily on plates, the gaily tripping fork goes *ping* when it hits the floor. Then comes the sound of a knife, a silent knife, always slicing meat, its brush against the plate barely audible. You only hear it when it's laid down again at the end of a meal, the grunt of a heavy handle that muffles any possible vibration of the blade. It's even more grotesque should it fall to the floor, *plaff*, like spoons, with no other rhythmic effect. What can the little drunkard be eating – the one who confused houses and got into theirs? Some fast food, no doubt, instantly prepared. Fried eggs with rice. No, that wouldn't require a knife. There's a knife and a fork, no question about that. He must be eating something out of those boxes delivered from outside, something you have to cut with a knife. There's a *pock* as a bottle is uncorked, liquid spilling into a familiar glass, his personal tall glass, as yellow as the bow round Belinda's neck.

Other sounds are of no interest. A chair scraping the floor when drawn back from the table, the jumbled confusion of glasses and plates being moved about, jars and drawers shut, bottles put away, until a demi-tasse spoon comes tinkling as it stirs sugar into coffee, making the beautiful sound of a child's spoon. Small spoons are far from unpleasant; they're sharp, they sing out, they're a good deal like singing forks.

Nabu's key-ring makes no sound of its own. It's a ragtag mix of knives and forks thrown into a box – old-fashioned big keys and small keys for modern locks jumbled together like knives and spoons; wardrobe and trunk keys, keys of odd shapes and sizes for all his boxes and instruments. A Nabu growing there in the middle of the room carries a pound or so of iron hanging from his belt.

Here, he says, not turning on his torch but reaching out in the dark, a salami sandwich in his hand. Old Aballay extends a palm, slowly groping so as not to brush the percussionist's fingers, then quickly eats. The kids stick out both hands, all at once, searching for the dark sandwich. Sila refuses it, saying she's not hungry, and Nabu tosses it on to the pillow. Cholo and Coca stretching out long hands, Kico too, all chewing as fast as they can, not degrading themselves. Hunger is free. The kids ask Sila whether she's going to eat or not. She gestures, reminding them that they must not speak, even in a low voice. Hadn't they heard the bell? And she begins chewing, with no other thought in her head. All of them chew in the dark, and another day draws to an end. Chewing under night-time regulation, something closely connected with Aunt Avelina's snapshot, which each of them carries deep inside, chewing, and it can't be unstuck – it would tear – Avelina's photograph beside the honeysuckle bush stuck in each of their heads. Avelina looks bigger and uglier now that they are on the other side, with the enemy, smack in the middle of the war uncovered by the percussionist.

Kico remembered the time he was spanked as a boy and locked himself in his room, wanting to die. That way they'd find out who he was and would weep with remorse. He had stopped up his nose and mouth with his hands. Impossible to breathe, death will come. He tried as hard as he could and then, taking in one more bit of air, he tried again. This time I must hold on to the end, I'm blacking out, it's coming, hold on a little more and it will be here. But he couldn't, his lungs were powerful lords who unblocked his mouth from inside and forced him to gulp large mouthfuls of pure air, until he fell asleep thinking of the tremendous power of the lungs.

Now he thought that that power was not so great. Older and stronger, he was in a position to take on these powerful lords with less primitive tactics than stopping up his nose and mouth. Now he could say no to life – that word whose symbol he'd made up himself – the same as saying no to a sandwich in spite of hunger. No, and that's that. What lay ahead of him was Nabu and his logic with keys, a future of paper-bird cut-outs. And you could not tell how old Nabu was in terms of years. He hovered between degrees of agedness, and that's where his chronology began. The kind of wounds that home remedies do not heal. And each step Nabu took, as with the spoon, meant the opening of new wounds. That was all that lay ahead, and Kico had no time for it; anyway, the roads were cut off. Behind him, of course, was a ravine.

Less than zero, nothing behind or ahead. Less than a photograph fading with age. Less than the snapshot of Tite blowing up a balloon that no longer exists, the absurdity of Tite appearing at Carnival, at parties with his ephemeral balloon. Less than all that, nothing behind or ahead, amid the sound of keys and the percussionist's nocturnal footsteps.

What about the others? We love you so much, Coca had told him, using new words. Don't say goodbye to them. When setting off on a long journey, it's best to leave quietly, very early, and let others sleep. It would be absurd to wake someone up to say, right, I'm off. When everyone else wakes, one should be gone, just like that. In the end, it's a matter of facing straight into the wind; the vicuña does not breed in captivity. After all, he wasn't losing much. Just three or four things, that was all – he, Kico, a small life made of small things, of hoped-for rather than real things. Stop up your nose and your mouth as you did as a boy, but in another way. There not much difference between what he might have killed then and what he could kill now. Previously, a few birthday parties with guests and always the same presents; now, a number of birthday parties more, these too the same, an album filled with the same picture card, for he never got any of the ones that were hard to come by. He had nothing to say except one or two irrelevant things. He was someone who never opened his mouth in a conversation, having nothing important to say. Then he'd better go and let others speak; they probably had things to dredge up. Even if he found words, he had little to say. He would leave a gathering while no one noticed, while others were laughing at a joke. He let no one ask why he was leaving so early, for he had nothing to explain either.

Even before Nabu's arrival Kico had begun to sense the darker side of what is meant by the word *life*. But he did not see it clearly at the time; he was draped in a cloth made of things that are hoped for but not yet there. Hope for one of the scarcer cards with the chocolate bar so as to complete his album and win the bicycle pictured on the cover. It was true that when you tore away the paper you almost always got the same card – a football player dancing with the ball in the middle of the field. But when you least expected it, there was also a motorcycle racer or a film star who used Palmolive soap, and you'd rush to stick the new card in your album, or one of the hard ones would turn up – a bolero singer, the inventor of the telephone, or something similar. But Nabu exposed that side, tearing the cloth off to reveal flesh covered by skin, with a wound beneath it. The hard-to-come-by cards did not exist, and you had to fill your album with the same duplicates. The chocolate bars sent to Hualacato only contained the card with the footballer in the middle of the field. There was another reason for this. The bike on the cover did not exist either; the percussionist had just proved it. It was Nabu who now took the place of the cards that were hard to find and the album cover; Nabu and the other side were one and the same thing – the wound. The other side had always been there, awaiting the percussionist's arrival, and now that he was there, before and after were the same. I have to hang on, I'm getting woozy, it's coming, it's close, just hang on a bit longer and that'll do it. The party's too boring, I've nothing to say, I'm leaving by the back door so nobody will notice, and I'll jump the ravine and face into the wind. I won't fill my album, not even with duplicates, especially as I know the bike's a lie invented to sell more chocolate. After all, a lot of Kicos are dying in Hualacato. And each Kico is barely three or four things of no importance, nothing to say at a party. He had coined a new word for life and now he had to give it up.

There was a sound like knocking, footsteps, a jangling key-ring, something breaking, or a nightly tour of inspection, but if you listened hard it was more of a drum beat, fingertips running lightly over the old man's door as Belinda, leaping through the transom and barely touching the floor, broke into a fast trot over the furniture and old hat boxes, and now the *click* of the transom as she exits. Only once do her feet touch down on the zinc roof, and there she is, clinging to the weathercock, the sound of her paws blending into the usual night sounds.

Like the baby of legend abandoned by the roadside in a wicker basket, the first feline breaks into a nasal caterwauling, in itself unbearable, only to be joined at once by a second, which yowls with something incurable, at the same time as a litter of motherless kittens lets loose. Both sides of the road are strewn with baskets of abandoned babies, and the broken glass set on the walls is filled with ears and wailing at the very moment the chorus living in the trees – the saddest, most plaintive orphans – joins in with those on the roof to provoke a veritable Slaughter of the Innocents in the thick of which Nabu dashes out, nerves frayed, running into the middle of his madness like a flare that illuminates half Hualacato, picking out cats with his various lights, staring at cats that switch on and off.

Just then Kico finds out that the hard-to-come-across card is Aunt Avelina and that by getting it he might even force the bike into existence. To make things make sense, always try the impossible.

Compressing his body and feeling that a few parts of it were unnecessary, that an ear folded back and flattened against the frame did not ease his head through the transom, that an elbow that refused to bend more than bone allowed was coming between him and the hard-to-get card, he finally managed to jump down on the other side, where he fell to the floor of the corridor that led to the living room and to Nabu's room. Rather than on a real floor he was placing his feet down on the fearful pages of the night regulations, with alarms and traps – that's where Kico was treading, carrying his three or four randomly chosen things and not hearing the sound of fear coming through the other transoms or that of his own fear, all of which was drowned out by the cries of disembowelled cats and Nabu running up and down out in the yard at the foot of the walls. In the traps set by regulation he left one at a time the three or four things in his possession – the birthday parties, the presents that lasted for one day, his only visit to the sea (almost faded from memory now), the duplicate cards, the dim and stupid image of the footballer dancing with the ball in the middle of the field, the cover of the album showing the happy faces of children admiring an imaginary bicycle. He was scrunched up as if he were losing himself but felt he was at last making space for reality, that suddenly a spoon was turning into a spoon again and flesh was covered by skin. As soon as he had the difficult card within reach, before and after would be joined again, connected by him, Kico. When he opened the percussionist's door, Kico felt he was touching the world – the real world whisked away by sleight of hand on the covers of an album.

With the last little thing left him he opened the folder of photographs, holes punched in them, each with a seal and a number. Smack in the centre of Roque's picture, right on the sumptuous volumes of the rented bookshelves, a huge oval seal hid the names of Roque's favourite authors and blotted one edge of his sumptuous cape. In almost all the photos of Aunt Francisquita's wedding there were question marks and arrows pointing to different faces. And on the best picture, the big 7 × 10 one, where she's alone in her white dress, an enormous cross of suspicion at the level of her embroidered bodice, the same as the postcards, also marked out as suspicious. And photos long since forgotten and not kept in boxes but distributed all about the house, now carefully filed and numbered – the ones of the zoo, for instance, silly pictures taken alongside a giraffe or begging bear, the old man and his compadre sitting on a bench like two perfect strangers in front of the lions' cage, surrounded by kids in bonnets holding balloons, possibly the crowning moment of a baptism or some such party. And the ones of Sila's fifteenth birthday, all in one pile – group photos, it seems, were very important to Nabu – also covered with arrows and question marks. Bocha by Sila's side, with his buck teeth and criminal face, making you wonder why he had no suspicious cross. With the crosses and seals, they all looked like criminals. Twenty years of life and crime in a blue folder. He riffled through them like the pages of a book, seeing how images assumed life and movement, in one second several years going by in faces barely glimpsed, terrified, surprised by the percussionist in the silence of their boxes. From the whirring pages the honeysuckle appeared and disappeared, just as the cats began to quieten down and from the bedrooms came coughing and whispers telling him he should pack it in, please, Kico, come back, the cats are finishing and Nabu will be back any minute now, night-time regulations, please get out of there, you'll have other chances to recover the photo, the sound of fear is unbearable now that the cats have gone silent. Riffling through the snaps again, Kico's thumb got stuck on the honeysuckle like on a letter in the dictionary, and Aunt Avelina stood there looking at him from her number. She didn't seem the same; she was enigmatic, neither laughing nor serious, as if the hand hidden behind her back was holding a fistful of razor blades, as if her full face and profile wanted on railway platforms were staring at him from the picture of Aunt Avelina's changed face with its number, 195, on the right-hand side. Tearing a picture to pieces always makes an impression; a bit of atavistic witchcraft being put to work. Hualacato's elderly would never let themselves be photographed. No way, they say. This can shorten our life, pins can be stuck in our eyes. Nothing doing. Put your camera away. Of course, it's not easy to tear up Aunt Avelina's picture, folding it like a paper bird, the hardened emulsion makes a horrible sound when it cracks. Aunt Avelina in tiny pieces, hidden between Kico's sock and his foot as he crosses the living room, breaking all rules, recovering presents and birthday parties. The musical top can still be heard, even if its string is broken. Aunt Avelina, stuffed inside his sock, slips through the transom just as heavy drops begin to pelt down on the zinc roof, pause for a moment in the little channels, from which they drip dully to the ground, and once again cats in disgrace rain on to the roof of the house, just as Nabu lies on his cot once more and turns off the lights, and an electric Belinda watches him from her hiding place in the middle of the begonias.

7

I HAVE A TELEGRAM HERE with a number of pro-
visional arrangements that will be to your benefit. According to the communication, this is – apparently – not a
dangerous family, as was initially believed and acted upon.
To be classified now as merely under suspicion will entail
a good deal of change. It means in the first place that you
can go on living in Hualacato and in this house, just as you
have been doing. Your worst crime, it would seem, has
been your participation in the noise strike, the subversive
nature of which I have proved to you beyond any doubt.
That comprised an act of resistance which, as you all know
full well, we shall eradicate at whatever cost. Personally, I
believe that the new label of suspect rather than dangerous
person is more the result of generosity than of a cold
analysis of strict fact. To me, you are still potentially
dangerous. I can read it in your faces, in what you swallow,
in your total indifference to everything. The goals to be
achieved are many, and in this house we are still far from
achieving them. Remember also that you should have
voluntarily requested my presence and you did not. That
is a capital sin. Had you done otherwise you might now be
leading normal lives, like most people in Hualacato. The
day you lot fit in, I shall be able to leave. But let us say

that from here on, owing to the new classification, relations between you and me will be less tightly controlled. The telegram authorises me for the time being to lift your incommunicado status. Within certain limits you will be allowed to speak on general subjects, without raising your voices, for you know my nerves are easily frayed. Let's get on to the contents of this telegram, with which, I warn you, I am not in general agreement. You had two breaks a week inside the house. From now on you'll be allowed outside into the patio and the garden, subject to one or two obvious restrictions. As from next week you'll go back to work, a factory lorry will pick you up at the door every morning and bring you back in the evening. Your two eldest children will work there too. The factory has expanded its facilities, and they need more people. Are there any questions?

'When does the outdoor break start?'

'Tomorrow, from five o'clock.'

'What'll the weather be like?'

'Wonderful, señora. Listen, those are birds singing.'

No, we should get the kids dressed first; that way they'll let us get on without interruptions. Let Grandad have his bath before anyone else and keep the kids away from the bathroom or they'll never stop knocking at the door. Meanwhile, you and I can start the ironing. Ironing? We have to find the clothes first. Everything's upside down. With every inspection things got scattered about. The other day I was looking for a shoe and it finally turned up in the kitchen – amongst the potatoes. I'm not counting the things he's still keeping, my leather handbag's been locked up in his desk drawer since the day he got here. We'd better iron Grandad's striped shirt and a sweater, just in case. And let's not forget hats for everyone. The sun may be very hot and it could be dangerous being exposed to it all at once. I've seen your sun hat squashed at the bottom of the trunk. If we starch and press it you'll be fine in it again. Shall I wear this summer dress? If the sun's too hot I can carry a parasol. That's the summer dress he made you take off that day. Señora, take that dress off. You're right; I'd forgotten. In that case I can wear my green dress. But that's a party dress, and we're only going out into the patio. It'll be like a party to me. I'm going to put on powder and rouge, eyeshadow, a touch of lipstick, and I'll do up my nails. And my bracelet, even if it's only to water the plants. I'd like Kico to wear his navy trousers, he looks so good in blue, and a short-sleeved white shirt. No, I think he should wear his yellow polo shirt with the little crocodile on the pocket. Then we'd better sprinkle all the clothes. And look for Cholo's sandals, the sun may cure his fungus. And don't forget to comb the kids' hair, we don't want to put something like that off till the last minute. It'll be like a party for them too. If I could I'd pack a basket with rolls and soft drinks, as if we were going on a country outing. He said the weather's wonderful. I'd love to take a photographer along to snap us looking happy. Cholo says we shouldn't be either happy or grateful, because we're not getting anything that isn't ours. But I don't know, to get out after all this time and see plants and the sun, who's going to be able to hide his feelings? Sila, please, can you do something with my hair? They won't know me when I step through that door.

You may come out, said Nabu from the patio. Cholo pushed a dimly remembered and now suddenly familiar door, its paintwork cracked, the small nail protruding on the right-hand side still there, and held it open for the old man to pass through on his wheels. Hit by the glare, old

Aballay covered his pained eyes. Come on, come on, let
the others out too, Nabu said. The kids queued up, hands
shading their eyes. They flocked to the middle of the patio,
huddled like peasants dumped in a strange city and taking
care not to get lost. Eyes shaded, they blinked at the trees
and walls and household appliances as if they were the
skyscrapers of the capital. What clods, thought the percussionist, seeing them knotted together as though someone
were about to take their picture at the zoo. A cat couldn't
have licked their hair down more neatly. Nabu took in
Coca's ridiculously long dress and stylish hair-do; the little
ones looking ready for a parade; Cholo's hopeless face,
which would spoil any clothing, any colour (in evening
dress or rigged up as an apache he'd always be the same);
the old man's absurd bow tie and winter hat, his Indian
face that smelled of rawhide and that he'd nicked while
shaving, his features which – Coca apart – were repeated
from Cholo to Julito. Nabu seemed to be seeing them for
the first time, as if he had just discovered that they too
were people.

'Look at the butterfly!' Coca shouted.

'It's just like a paper cut-out,' said one of the kids,
shielding his eyes.

Julito, to whom two new things happened that day – he
both began to walk and saw the sun – uncovered his eyes
to have a look but shut them at once, wrinkling up his
nose. The butterfly disappeared over the wall, a piece of
paper blown away by the wind.

'Do I have to tell him I want to go to the garden shed
for the pruning shears?' Kico asked his father.

'I don't think so. He let us out, so I imagine he wants us
to move around. We can't just stand about all afternoon
like fools.'

Kico went to the shed, passing very close to Nabu, who

was stationed strategically – as he had been indoors at the centre of the house – under his own sun umbrella. Lying in a hammock that was a little the worse for wear owing to exposure to the elements, he leafed through a magazine, and there was no *click* when Kico moved past him or when he returned with a saw blade.

'This is all I could find. All our tools are locked up. He's locked everything up.'

As their eyes adjusted to the sun they lowered their hands from their brows, and the things they'd been forced to abandon now looked like statues in a park. The wheelbarrow; the chicken coop's little roof; the lemon tree; the garden shed's brick wall; the boundary wall, whose three new rows of brick already had a patina like the rows below; the broken bottles – they were all statues disfigured by time. The unfamiliar sun made the Aballays blink, but gradually objects took on their old familiar shapes. Still clustered together in a group, the family stared at things, pointing a finger at them and naming them – the wall, the wooden gate, the peach tree – tourists coming off the train and pointing like fools at the cathedral, the bridge, the palace of mirrors, public monuments. And that was the end of it, a long journey just to see three or four silly things.

'You can start chopping weeds,' said the percussionist. 'And if you come across any dead cats, bury them.'

The business about everything being as it always was simply is not true. Things can become familiar again, but they are different. Their old appearance is kept up as a form of piety, but they are hollow, they belong to the past. They have projected their appearance on to the future so as to give the illusion of a continuity they no longer have. Waxwork dummies. The real object stands there, irretrievable. The wheelbarrow, upside down since the afternoon of the night of the percussionist's arrival, no longer exists despite the fact that it's still there, a bit rustier and in the same place. The real wheelbarrow has stayed behind, abandoned, and all this time has been projecting its image to all Hualacato so as to be somewhere and to help keep up an appearance of reality. Between the wheelbarrow and himself, Cholo knew by intuition, was a lapse of time that life and the wheelbarrow both missed, since wheelbarrows as well as men exist because of continuity. Time has moved on, the world has moved through space it will never again occupy. The wooden gate looks the same. Pure illusion, for Yeyo has never passed through that gate again, to mention but one example. These objects are like bad negatives now. No matter what tricks we get up to in the darkroom, we'll never get a perfect image, and they will always come out either too dark or too light. Among the weeds the bones of hens and chicks lie bleaching. Thirst, hunger, anything. The wind has blown the feathers away. The garden shed, the wooden gate, the wheelbarrow, and everything else are chicken bones. The only difference is that the hens were unable to make a pretence of continuity and dropped dead. These are illusory appearances, like the photographs of the dead that are placed on graves when below ground not even the wood of their coffin is left.

'Cholo, can you bring me the wheelbarrow, please?' asked Coca. 'We'll get rid of all these chicken bones first, then cut the weeds to make it easier for Julito to walk. I'll water the plants.'

Coca spoke as if everything was the same as it had been, whereas to Cholo the wheelbarrow felt dead.

'I don't want to touch it,' he said, embarrassed. 'It's not the same wheelbarrow as before.'

'I don't understand you,' she complained, waiting for a clearer explanation. Her eyes registered disbelief.

'It was the last thing I touched before he arrived,' Cholo said, trying to explain what he couldn't.

'What a shame. Looks like it's going to get cooler. I should have brought my bed jacket,' Coca said, digging out the legs of the wheelbarrow, which immediately filled with children.

Indifferent to objects, the old man ran up and down the garden, his wheelchair appearing and disappearing behind shrubbery and suddenly stopping in the areas the others cleared of weeds. He muttered and looked up, searching for his old birds. Instead of turning the wheels by hand he cranked the chair along, which allowed him to flit about at great speed. Nabu noticed old Aballay avoiding stones and holes and adjusting to the rough ground. It was incredible how the old man handled his chair. With a tinful of seeds from the garden shed or from the wheelchair he made a fool of himself, shaking it and making bird sounds, muttering under his breath or talking baby talk. But the birds didn't come near, as they once had; they didn't recognise him in his scarecrow hat and absurd little bow tie.

'You there,' said Nabu, pointing to Sila, 'go and get those books on the shelf.'

There were some fifty books in the house, all unread. Some had been bought at news-stands, others had been borrowed or had been given as gifts. Whatever the case, they were objects linked to people and memories. The book telling a story of a solitary voyager was – more than a book – also the little blue ribbon with which Aunt Marcelina had brought it as a present, a ribbon that was still somewhere in one of the cabin trunks.

'Even if I haven't read them,' the old man said, 'even if they're bad books, there must be something good in them.'

'I haven't even glanced at the titles,' said Nabu, lighting

a match. 'What we're burning here – I'm telling you this for your own good – is delusions. Funny notions.'

Julito marvelled at the mechanism of the fire, screaming with joy, as if being dipped into the sea for the first time.

'Is this a bad book too?' asked Sila, pointing to a copy of *Photography for Everyone*, which was giving off a cloud of smoke.

'I've said I haven't even glanced at the titles. I have no idea what's good or bad – nor do I care. How many dead cats did you come across?'

'None,' Cholo said. 'Cats never die at home. When they're injured or ill they take themselves off to die in the woods.'

'Come with me, the lot of you,' said the percussionist.

It was the first time he turned his back to them. They looked at each other, apprehensive, communicating by signs, bewildered, haunted by the shadow of Aunt Avelina.

'I see it hasn't dawned on you yet what your change of classification means. We're all under suspicion until the moment we prove otherwise. But the dangerous person – unlike the one who is merely under suspicion – is beyond redemption. I haven't seen one of you looking happy yet. Perhaps you don't want to live in Hualacato any more. Do you know what you're going to do now? Cheer up. From day one I said I wanted to see happy faces. And I want to see them today. Right now. Your recreation periods were designed for that. Otherwise they'll be taken away from you.'

'It's not easy just to turn it on. Maybe we could sing something,' Coca said.

'I wasn't referring to you. I really meant your husband and your two eldest. They dress up as for a party and put on faces for a funeral. Let's have a look and see if you can live in Hualacato,' he said to Cholo. 'Can you tap-dance?'

'No, sir.'

'Come on, being your father's son you should know how. You should know lots of things. Everyone can do something unusual. The kind of things you do at a party. Singing, reciting poems, tap-dancing, clowning, animal imitations, magic tricks – whatever.'

'I can't do any of those things.'

'I'm ordering you to.'

Self-conscious about how ridiculous he looked, Cholo made a stab at it, but he did not know how to dance and there was no music. He shuffled about, staring at the wheelbarrow and gate, under whose pious shapes death lay in waiting. He remembered Tite, dead, appearing in the course of one Carnival, and tears sprang to Cholo's eyes. Twice he brought his dance to an end; twice Nabu ordered him to go on.

'You're doing quite well,' said Coca.

'Wonderful,' said the old man.

'Go on, Dad, it's getting better all the time,' Kico and Sila told him.

On one side were the wheelbarrow, Tite, the worm-eaten gate. Cholo could go away, leaving these things behind, and from time to time send a picture of himself back to Hualacato to keep up illusions. That's what he wanted. On the other side were Coca, face powdered, and the kids with their hair combed jumping up and down on the wheelbarrow and encouraging him, and Kico and Sila, who had never been teenagers, telling lies like practised schoolteachers, go on, it's getting better all the time. What he'd done was not tap-dancing; it was running away from life in the shape of a wound, ridding his head of all funny notions so as to see only the wound. The percussionist was right. Up until now Cholo had been mistaken, because his head was full of strange ideas, but as he danced he began losing some of them. At his age learning to dance wasn't easy, yet he had no way out. The kids were alive, Coca powdered to the eyeballs, and they weren't letting him leave by the rotten gate. Nabu had locked the wheelbarrow, denying him that way out. Even the grave was padlocked. No before, no behind, so then what? The factory lorry arriving at dawn to take him tap-dancing, Kico and Sila, never teenagers, in the back of the lorry, they too going to tap-dance, everybody going, until the percussionists came. You're going to play, no question about that. We were on our way to Yeyo's for maize when they landed. They never fall back but are like nature's cycles, geological strata, animals in rut; they're the we're-sorry-but-there's-no-other-way, the timely-rain-would-have-cleared-the-whole-thing-up of the nurses at the hospital. We went to Aunt Francisquita's wedding and by the end of the party each of us began doing what we knew best. Coca mimicked film stars of the day and Bocha the croak of a frog. None of us knew that Nabu would arrive with his wounds, even without cotton wool he operates all the same, we'll do what we can opening his head to extract the funny ideas, the patient will recover, and you'll see him tap-dancing for sheer joy, because being alive is not easy, you have to know how to move your feet, adapt, adapt to smiling at life. Look at Coca, she's let her hair down, put on lipstick and a long dress, and come to a party, and you love your own skin even if it's a curtain, a backdrop hiding a wound, and you become aware of all this while still tap-dancing without music to mark the rhythm, tap-dancing until somebody says what a pity the toy's broken, the story's over, living is being in the middle of a room jumping about and clowning to show the guests that you can do something after all, but at the same time wishing you could slip out through that locked door, only there's nothing you can do but go on tap-dancing. That's it, Dad, you're getting the rhythm now, it's not right yet but you're getting there, that step was good but some of the others need work, there's plenty of time, life is long, you don't have to give up, the wheelbarrow and gate are full of deceit, don't be carried away by them, a little step forward and we can all travel, look, the front of the coach is empty, move forward please and fill up the front, make room for others otherwise we'll call the police, come on, let's see you tap-dance, come on, Cholo, you've got the rhythm and there's still plenty of time, go on, go on, shout the kids from the wheelbarrow, Cholo's pleased, thinking he's found his rhythm, the others know he hasn't but they say nothing, that's it, that's it, they say, it's wonderful, Cholo's saving himself and saving the rest of them, he's the head of the family, the little family head finally working his way into joy, into truth, into the wound, into the percussionist's icy heart, and when the tap-dance is over he's there inside.

Cholo was walking backwards through some deep tunnels. He no longer had any connection with life but was forced to go on living, he was there simply to prolong the others' lives. Maybe that's what the percussionist called the right rhythm. Cholo had no skin now, his whole body was flayed. Backwards, projecting his image into the future so that others might go on believing the world was still real. They'd still go on calling him Cholo, a word that made no sense now, as had happened with the word *spoon*. Spoon, noops, psnoo, Cholo, Locho, Olcho, anything at all and keep on tap-dancing to the very end, the ground will outlast you. And your skinned flesh, you couldn't even cover yourself with your hands because they were skinless too, so up in the air, backwards, meanwhile everything's all right, everyone's finding a way into Nabu's heart.

Cholo hears Sila and Coca singing as if from afar; Kico accompanies them on his guitar, and the old man on his reed. We've always been a bit silly about this sort of thing, Coca said. Never mind, just sing, said Nabu, and now they're singing without knowing what it's like in the percussionist's heart, that's why one's better off going backwards. Cholo was going backwards but the ground began moving the opposite way; he thought he was going backwards but was standing in the same place. This was the rhythm all right, stock-still in front of the percussionist. Unable to turn his back when they kept calling him Cholo or to touch the dead wheelbarrow (since words and thoughts no longer meant anything to him), he would have to be a master of sleight-of-hand to be able to turn his back on reality. Magicians needed words to change things, a tap of the wand and presto, three rabbits out of a hat.

'Your singing was good,' Nabu said, addressing them all. 'Now it's your turn.'

'I wouldn't know how to begin,' said old Aballay.

'Why don't you tell him that story about the horses?' Coca said, loosening his bow tie and taking his hat off to see whether it stopped his sweating.

'Come on, get started,' Nabu said.

The old man bathed the percussionist in a mild look that told of flocks and wheat fields. It was a quiet glance barely altered by the almost invisible glow of the sweet intelligence at play behind it. He was looking at Nabu in a way that made the others hold their breath in the expectation of seeing three rabbits pop out of the old man's hat, which he held in his hands. He gazed at Nabu in a pause, in a suspended silence, and his quiet look was one of an animal practising mimicry. More than a look, it was purposeful, a desire hidden in playful eyes, an act arrested in a glow that still lay in the future. Used to a different sort of perception, the percussionist's eyes were unable to understand or bear the sweetness of the flock and they turned away towards the flames of the fire.

'Begin at once. We haven't much time left.'

In some fields a long time ago, when those fields were ours, there were many lions.

The lion story again, the family thought, not without annoyance. Too well known that story – besides, all hunting stories are alike.

Being the lions that they were, the old man went on, they ate up the small animals we were breeding. A lion dines on his prey until he's glutted but always leaves part of his quarry uneaten – the lowly innards, say, something he can leave for a time of greater need. Following the habit of all lions (which is what a lion is supposed to do – that and nothing else), he buries these remains, if it is his intention to return, hiding the cache under leaves and stones. And off he goes. The wind will take care of the rest. Then, they too dissembling, trackers find the place as if by chance and without coming too close, casually, they build around the concealed remains a kind of stick fence that isn't really a fence and that can be mistaken for any other part of the wood. They leave the fence there like a door that's not quite a door, something that might have been shaped by the rain or wind, and in an unequivocal spot they set a trap, two iron jaws and a long chain. The trackers then slowly withdraw, covering over their own tracks, stepping almost without touching the ground, almost on tiptoe, flying like feathers in the wind so as to leave no trace of their smell. The beast, following the habit of lions and in order to go on being a lion, does not jump over the fence. He sees they've tried to conceal it and senses danger. And then enters the door that's not quite a door and, of course, there's the trap, the iron jaws clamping on to the lion's paws. That's when he gives a roar that wakes the dogs, the dogs wake the men, and the lion sets off through the wood, roaring and dragging the chain, in his fury opening up lanes through the undergrowth. But the chain becomes tangled in brambles, branches, thickets, uprooting some plants but not the whole wood, and now the lion can no longer run and the wood becomes a spider's web to him, and men are closing in on him with their hunting dogs and their sticks, which are also a habit that somehow fits the habits of lions.

Old Aballay abruptly cut off as if he had forgotten the rest of his story. Cholo could not bear the pity he felt for the old man, who was changing a familiar old story, choosing his words and charging them with meaning so as to create a spell. But it was a pointless game, and his words were as useless as needles stuck into photographs or candles lit in a wood in broad daylight to scare off evil spirits. Nabu didn't even hear him. He had dozed off.

He was an old lion who'd already eaten one of our mares and was looking for her foal, a little colt, which was a delicacy to him. We kept hiding the colt, moving it from place to place according to the direction of the wind, but the lion can smell a favourite snack from any distance, and at night we would hear his deliberate footsteps, his tail brushing past, his lion's mistakes – because they make mistakes too. Some nights we had to lock the colt up with us indoors. Hunger was forcing the lion to run his final risk. In the end we had to give Cascabel up to him. Cascabel was a young mule we fed to the lion so as to buy him off while our colt was growing. Unable to do anything, we saw the lion leap on Cascabel and drive one of his claws into the mule's mouth and twist his head aside so that Cascabel was running with the lion on top of him, not knowing where he was going, the claw-like reins that drove

Cascabel wherever the lion wanted. He drove the mule on until Cascabel dashed his head against a carob tree and was knocked out. Lions never disembowel an animal that is putting up a struggle. The animal has to be alive but motionless. Then the lion devoured all he could and buried the remains. On his return for them, you know what happened to him.

You can stop now, it looks like he's fallen asleep, Cholo said by signs, and using the same language the old man told Cholo not to interrupt.

When he heard the dogs barking, the lion scampered for the wood, dragging his chain. Not because he feared the dogs, obviously, but because he knew – as all lions know – that behind the dogs came men armed with sticks. Cornered, the lion sprang up into a hackberry tree, tearing off some of its branches with the chain. The dogs leapt as high as they were able, trying to bite the lion, but they could not reach him. The one that leapt highest, our best dog, was eviscerated by a single swipe of the lion's paw. It was a sorry sight to see the hound fall to the ground with nothing inside it. All its guts hung there, as high as the dog had jumped, like wet rags. The lion glowered at us, men and dogs, in a way that made us believe it would be impossible to get him down. It was as if the tree went up for ever and the lion could go on climbing it until he vanished. As though he himself believed this, he tried to leap to a higher branch but missed and began tumbling down, stunned as Cascabel had been, hitting the branches and snapping them off as he fell, lost in his own habits, dropping into the mouths of sticks and the dogs, falling like a pillar of fire. I could not watch how they finished him off and I went looking for some animal to carry the lion to where we did our skinning. The dogs were baying restlessly, watching out for the least movement the beast made as it lay dying, and their teeth bit into him whenever a leg or muscle twitched, but these were no longer voluntary motions. I couldn't bring my mule in close. He had only to smell the lion and he stood fast in his tracks. I stroked his back to steady him and felt the flesh trembling under his skin. I had to cover his head with a rag so he couldn't see or smell anything, and only that way could I lead him to where the lion lay, his habits at rest. All together we hoisted him up on to the mule, which had to walk blindly, led by the reins. The dogs followed along, on guard, tongues hanging out, tails erect, whimpering from time to time as their fear of the lion revived. The lion's front legs dragged along the ground on one side, his hind legs on the other, the claws leaving furrows in the sandy soil that remained there until the rain wiped them out.

'All right, you can go inside now,' Nabu said.

The group was huddled round the embers of the fire. It was growing dark, and suddenly the air turned cold. The old man blew on a half-burnt book and when a tiny flame flared he lit his pipe. He was sucking at it when they heard the percussionist blow his whistle to announce that the break was over.

8

ODD PEOPLE THESE TOURISTS, armed with walking sticks and cameras, devouring everything in sight, Kico thought as his eyes took in a town that seemed the same as ever except for a few streets cut off by lorries parked across the intersections and smack in the middle of a block, furniture piled high and people standing in queues, either moving out or thrown out. He was on his way to the milk bar just along the way for something to eat, but this was one of the places where people were moving house, recklessly it seemed, with chairs being thrown out of windows to crash down on a mound of furniture and to smash mirrors. Very odd these tourists, each dressed in the fashion of his or her own faraway country and almost more of them even than Hualacateños. To find another milk bar (he fancied a bowl of cereal with hot milk) meant walking a long distance, and he would not be back on time. So he'd better eat a sandwich somewhere close by. He'd seen a tourist inspecting the machine shop at the factory that morning on one of those tours that are a nuisance, since somehow when they're around you can't work comfortably. And the way they dress, Kico thought, loud colours, cameras and spyglasses hanging everywhere, wearing gloves and their heads disfigured by the cut of their hair, shaven at the back, a little fringe at the front, and the rest tied in a tuft on top that blows in the breeze. They have the hunter's look of a very primitive people, but close up those are not walking sticks. Although these people are in Hualacato as visitors, at the same time they have brought blowguns along.

It was hard to see everything in an hour, not counting the ten minutes it would take to eat a sandwich and the time lost crossing the factory's big yards. In fact, he had only thirty minutes left in which to get to know the town again after so many months. Thirty minutes a day, but if he picked a different street each time he could take in quite a bit, even if he had to restrict himself to the neighbourhood of the factory.

Hurrying along, Kico lost his way. At a corner he only dimly remembered, traffic had been cut off and he had to turn left into what he thought was a little street with fast-food bars. Instead, he was heading back to the factory. It could be said that this was his first day in Hualacato, in the world, in life after having failed some years earlier in his attempt to stop breathing by holding a hand over his mouth and nose. Birthday parties and musical tops were over and done with; today, in long trousers and in his small way, he was strolling along, a bit lost, on a pavement that allowed him to enter what's known as life. Neither boy nor man, he was what Aunt Marcelina referred to as 'such a little man', and inside his pocket he pressed his identity card against his leg. The percussionist had recommended he carry it when he left for work, a piece of paper without which you could not live in Hualacato or anywhere else, a piece of paper that proved there was nothing odd about him, that he had given up the idea of not breathing, that he was there of his own accord and had understood the explanations he had been given, which was why he was alive, even if at present life was worth very little. On his birthday, a bit scared, no funny ideas in his head, Kico was walking towards what his aunts called the future. Of the two pavements, he felt one was for love and the other for cannibalism. A throng of people and vehicles, obviously a collision or someone who had forgotten his papers or most likely of all another lot moving house, forced him to go down another street, which had only one pavement. The one opposite had been removed, and the roadway ran right to the dirty foot of the buildings on that side. He walked down the middle of the street so as to avoid the single pavement, convinced that it was the one for cannibalism. After all, everything in town had a cannibal air about it, otherwise what were those weirdo tourists with the blowguns and tufts of hair and the huge spyglasses doing there.

The morning had been very long, proving the truth of one of Nabu's sermons, according to which life could be quite long if you were careful to mark its passage. The day began with a lorry idling by their doorstep while it was still dark, and he and Sila climbed in alongside their father while Nabu handed the driver some papers. Others in the vehicle had huddled up to make room for them, in silence, saying neither good morning or anything else. Kico now understood what Nabu meant by the word *emaciated*. The silent, long-suffering faces seemed to have come from the back of beyond. Sila was the only woman present; seeing this, the others – all emaciated men – made still more room so she could hold on to one side of the lorry's loading platform and avoid being jostled on the drive to the factory. His father rode at the far end, and excusing himself without any verbal response from those around him – though they all pressed up tight to let him squeeze by – he drew up to Cholo to say a few words. He looked happy. The clean early morning air felt good on his wan face. But going back to work was more than the joy of being able to leave home as if he were free; it also meant finding again the little road he had made for himself in the world since he began breathing on his own. He was a tiny ant who in twenty years of coming and going had made his own small way to the factory and eventually felt affection for his tools and ladders. He can't leave this little road, because it's the only one he has; the ant would get lost and not know where to turn, and life's not long enough to find another road. Ants don't live long, which is why he tap-dances all the way to his ant hill every day. He didn't like it. The happiness he felt at being able to leave home and see Hualacato again vanished in the back of the lorry as it turned down dark streets, knocking the emaciated men into one another. The outlandish size of the factory, its vast machine shops, its signboards (like those hung by Nabu, pretending they were walls) written in a language that was not the language spoken in Huala-cato did not help either. Nor did the fact that his father, dwarfed by the machines as he disappeared high up on them carrying a handful of rags, could not be seen from below. The ant hill was too big; the factory went on below ground in a series of endless cellars, all full of men, machines, and oil rags. It was impossible to calculate its size above ground either, with its many floors and warm, secret offices. He had no idea where they had put Sila, up or down like him. He was trying to familiarise himself with a vast quantity of iron in shapes he had never dreamed of. To steady himself, he pictured his sister as a lift operator, sitting prettily on her stool, switching levers, saying up, down, and switching levers until she reached the very top of the ant hill, opening a little way for herself so as not to get lost.

He had made his way more than half a block down the street with the single pavement, certain that on the next corner there'd be a bar where he could eat a sandwich and come straight back as there was little time left. But from that direction came no fewer than six tourists, chatting absent-mindedly, waving their walking sticks about, and taking up the whole width of the road, one of them looking through his spyglass. Kico turned abruptly, about to run, just as the first whistle blew at the factory. He had ten minutes and still must cross that vast yard, which would take at least half that time. Anyway, the factory had a canteen or sandwich machine. Turning his back on the tourists, who were walking faster than one would expect, he headed straight for the factory, looking up at its huge tower, which could be seen from all over town. His trousers rushed down the street. Goodness, how time had flown.

Hesitating at the corner, looking for the tower, which was now nowhere in sight, lost in this changing town, he spotted a milk bar that hadn't been there before. How can this be, I just passed by here? Should he stop for a glass of milk and risk being late, the last whistle surprising him as he took his first sip? Or should he press on and arrive in the nick of time, knowing machines do not wait?

'Where are you coming from? Let's see your papers. Is anything wrong? Are you lost? Are you all right? Or do you need something?'

'No, nothing. I was just looking for a place to get a bite to eat.'

'Restaurants are that way,' said the tourist, pointing his walking stick towards the bottom of the street.

'But traffic's been cut off at the next corner.'

'That way, then.' The walking stick pointed in the other direction.

'As a matter of fact,' Kico said, 'I only wanted a glass of milk.'

'Where do you work?' the tourist said, drawing near, his tuft of hair blowing slightly in the breeze.

'At the factory. I came out for lunch and got lost. A lot of the streets have been closed, and people are moving house.'

'Then you haven't much time; the first whistle has already sounded,' said the tourist. He handed Kico's papers back and continued his stroll, one hand on his camera, the other swinging his walking stick rhythmically.

Better get back to the factory, they'll surely let him into the canteen. The trouble is, I got lost, he'd tell them. So as not to be late I've had no lunch. I wouldn't dream of causing any trouble here. Not to worry, lad. Let's see, who can fill in for the lad here so he can get to the canteen; he hasn't had his lunch. The lad. The little man. And before long my face will be emaciated too. He was right in the middle of his first day of intelligent life, according to the percussionist's definition. But Kico had never talked to anyone about the changes, all these closed streets and people moving away. He was moving away too, becoming someone who no longer had much to do with Kico. Everybody, not only furniture, was moving. People were moving into other people, into other bodies. Tourists were not tourists, they were just people on the move. At least half of Hualacato was moving away. Any day now the percussionist would shave the back of their heads, leave a plume on top, and furnish everyone with a blowgun. We'll begin to lose our eyesight and have to use spyglasses; we'll lose our memories and have to go around taking photographs to remember anything. I don't remember anything. I got lost in the centre of Hualacato, and soon nobody will recognise anyone else. I've come to save you, and you'll have to play, rest assured of that. And I want to see some joy on those emaciated faces. The trouble is you know a lot but you keep it all to yourselves. Which is reflected in your faces, otherwise you'd be living quietly like so many others in Hualacato. When everyone had the back of their heads shaven close and used their blowguns to hunt down others, the percussionist would go home. There'd be a big farewell party. The task hasn't been easy, but now it's finished. And so, brothers and sisters, we each turn to other things; you must live as you should, your heads empty of any funny ideas; goodbye, I embrace you all. Please write. I'll be seeing you. Goodbye, goodbye, and forgive me if I ever went too far. It was for your own good. When the kids grow up, they'll thank me for it. Cholo, come here and let me embrace you; that's it, like brothers. After all, isn't each of us a Hualacateño? Do you people not realise how things have changed in such a short time? And to think that you used to be afraid of me. Fear, between brothers. And these are my farewell gifts – a blowgun for each of you to remember me by.

A block before he reached the factory he noticed that one of the tourists or hunters had slipped out of a house and was following him. Better slow his step so his pursuer wouldn't think Kico was trying to elude him. Kico felt the man close, as if he had eyes at the back of his head. Changes.

'Kico,' called the hunter, coming alongside. The voice was Cachimba's.

A changed face, a plume of hair, a face made of scars, the nape of his neck shaven close, a blowgun in his hand – there was not much of Cachimba left. Only his voice was the same, the unmistakable way he said Kico.

'I hope you won't be afraid to recognise me,' he said, laying a hand on Kico's arm. 'I'm Cachimba.'

'*So huving yourself Cachimba, eh?*'

'We have to be in touch. There's so much. We're fighting back.'

'I'm afraid,' Kico said. 'We had a snapshot of Aunt Avelina at home.'

'Did my clothes frighten you? Dressing like a hunter's the only way of getting around in the open. We know you have outdoor breaks now. One day soon you'll be getting messages from the compadre.'

'*Good heavens, Cachimba and Uvelina.*'

'I can see how frightened you are. I'm leaving now. See you soon.'

'How's Aunt Avelina?'

'She's dead, like so many others,' Cachimba said hurriedly, disappearing inside a house.

The sound that whistle makes, he said to himself on his way down the ant hill's stairs. He tried to make as much noise as possible with his feet so no one would hear his fear.

Pity it was night again, otherwise they could have seen the whole southern part of Hualacato from the avenue along which the lorry was returning. The three of them clung to the sides of the loading platform, hypnotised by the lights of the town. Look! Cholo said, Aunt Francisquita's house. What would she be up to at that moment, amongst her little coffee cups, her embroidered doilies, and her Carlos? What was her percussionist like? She had one, of course, her windows were covered over with black pasteboard. Poor Auntie, in mourning again. And the geraniums in her garden thirsty for water in a thicket of weeds.

Nabu was waiting for them on the pavement. Three, he said to the driver. He pushed open the front door without a word to them. Sila patted the door as if it were a live animal. They stared at the front of the house, up at the barely visible weathercock, gawking in amazement. Nabu held the door open and shouted *quiet!* to a big black bulk that was rolling about inside.

'This dog will be living with us from now on,' Nabu said. 'He is restless because he can't find the cat. So call her, let them get to know each other, and if they must we'll let them fight. They're going to have to learn to live together. You'll show this animal respect, for he too has authority. And watch out, he's been carefully trained. Now stand over there so he can sniff and get to know you. That way there'll be no problems. He's already had a noseful of the others, and everything's fine.'

The percussionist snapped his fingers, and immediately the dog was sniffing Cholo just as if he were frisking him. Cholo's shoes, pockets, every fold of his trousers, his buttons, his bottom, his crotch – the damp muzzle was everywhere, sniffing nervously, discovering bits of fluff and traces of oil from the factory. To reach higher, the dog raised his paws to Cholo's chest and then up to his shoulders and sniffed; Cholo lifted his arms and, whimpering, the animal's nose ran over his hair, the back of his neck, his mole, and a couple of neck scars, nothing there, and the muzzle leapt over to Sila. She turned, and the muzzle, like myriad hands, began giving Sila's body its first feel – nothing here either. The animal was almost placid now. Kico's back is splotched, measles again, red spots, when once more the dog starts sniffing him all over and begins growling. He scorns Kico's lower parts and paws his chest, his nose twitching nervously as the dog sniffs the arm touched by the late Aunt Avelina's husband. The animal hesitates, seeking new places, but keeps returning to the arm, to traces of the scent of the disguised tourist's fingers. The dog's muzzle is at work, frantic, growling, baring his antediluvian teeth, waiting for a command to sink them into the hateful smell.

The percussionist called the dog off with a less intense snap of the fingers, then stared at Kico out of thousand-year-old eyes – first at the boy's face and then his arm as the dog whimpered in a corner. Face screwed up, eyes narrowed, the percussionist scrutinised a black wall, looking for some connection. He was thinking, as if inhaling air deeply, and as he let his breath out his thoughts ran over the wall, searching for something over or beneath it, something that connected Kico to the dog's memory, but Nabu's air was nearly finished and he came up with nothing, no opening in the wall to let light through.

'Very strange,' said Nabu after exhaling, and he stood there staring ahead of him absent-mindedly. 'Has anything happened to your arm?'

'Last night Belinda came into my room and spent the whole night lying against it.'

'Bring me the cat, then,' said the percussionist, unconvinced.

'Belinda!' called old Aballay, and the cat, materialising out of thin air, sat like a begonia pot, as was her habit, and remained still, except for her tail, which bristled and covered part of her face, so that only her eyes could be seen as they changed from dark spheres to yellow rhombuses.

They looked at each other greedily, the dog with fiery but evidently domesticated eyes, the cat's with a touch of the primitive in them, yet in their way sweet. The dog began working himself into a rage by circling the cat, while she – her body still in the flower-pot position – followed him with her eyes, then with a quarter turn of the head, after which, not to lose sight of the black bulk, the moment the dog was behind her she stuck her head between her paws and looked at him from an upside-down position, her head close to the floor. The dog saw the cat with her mouth above her eyes, which almost distracted him from the backward kick that the cat was preparing but never let loose, since the dog quickly put distance between them and got out of range. The dog turned, exploring, and again was in front of Belinda, who had gone back to her original position, hiding part of her face with her tail. From Nabu's mouth came a monosyllabic command, and the black bulk made space to leap, eyes fixed on the cat, which, in her uneasy stillness, looked like a plaster sculpture. The cat heard the dog's claws scrape the floor as it was about to leap, and when she saw him up in the air she shifted her electric body into different positions, showing him at least two illusory Belindas. In the midst of his leap the dog chose the image that seemed more real to him and went for it with every fibre of his muscle and bone. He landed off to one side of Belinda, who appeared not to have stirred an inch.

'Excellent move on the cat's part,' Nabu remarked. Familiar with the swiftness of felines, he had caught Belinda's manoeuvres and he gave the dog another command.

Hearing it, the dog launched into a zigzag leap at the cat's shifting images, relying more on geometric chance than on the reality before his eyes. The target of his teeth was Belinda's head. This ensured that he could get at the cat's body a couple of times, without having to single it out beforehand, and could bite into her back and tear off a couple of her teats. Nabu was now reconciled to the dog's handlers, who had at least taught the animal this.

Belinda took refuge under a chair. She had lost the harmony of her lines. Her fur, once like honeysuckle, looked like a bundle of straw, a heap of beaten rags, something that hangs from a branch. She was about to flee, unable to do anything other than concentrate her instinct so as not to lick her wounds and by doing so allow the black bulk to have a good nip at her head.

Seeing that the cat would not be distracted despite the blood that ran from her torn teats, the dog attempted one or two lunges and managed to get hold of the cat's loose bow, by which he pulled her out from under the protective legs of a chair. Risking another lunge, he left his hind quarters unprotected and was suddenly immersed in the unendurable pain caused by the three claws that had dug into his testicles. When he turned to lick at the pain, a perfectly aimed hook struck him in one eye. With the other he could just see that the cat, retracting her claws into a soft, secret sheath, was smoothing her fur and recovering her normal appearance, as contented and confident as a fisherman at the moment he pulls in his catch.

Upon his master's command, using his one good eye, the whimpering dog skulked off to Nabu's room. Belinda disappeared high up into some part of the house.

9

SUNDAY SERMONS WERE like boring movies. With long pauses between paragraphs and with words left dangling in mid-air, Nabu read slowly, reading and pacing between his unrooted words, which kept getting mired in the torpor brought on by his audience's slow digestion. Where words ended and his rhythmic pacing began a siesta of sorts intruded. Up and down the living room he paced, while the Aballays sat still in a semi-circle, nodding off, the kids occasionally falling sound asleep and sliding from their chairs. At first, owing to their Sunday regularity, these sermons were like calendars. It was the only day of the week when the kids did not ask what day it was, for Nabu's pacing and reading meant Sunday – except when something momentous took place outside the house, which they all sensed but had no real knowledge of and which resulted in unscheduled sermons at any time on any day of the week. What a boring Sunday, the kids would say, and it would be a Wednesday. That the children came to know weeks with three Sundays gives some idea of how time flew.

The sermons were like the collected lectures of a long, long science course, volume XVII, page 96, let's see who can review for us the fundamentals of last Sunday's sermon on the subject of history's great saviours, of which only a mixed bag – scraps of sleep, dreams, post-prandial sluggishness, and pointless evasions – remains. As they listened to Nabu they sometimes went to sleep or escaped by a landscape or situation suggested by his words, thereby becoming free in some other century, on some other latitude. Do you understand? Nabu would ask. Which was impossible, for they had not been there, they'd been journeying across the high seas, stowaways on some expedition, and had won freedom in the remote history of an even more remote country. A history of good guys and bad guys, in which the goodies were always the saviours and the baddies everyone else, pigeon holes containing the words *iconoclasts*, *bandits*, *perverts*, *sepoys*, *addicts*, *criminals*, *traitors*, and *Cachimbas*. In their meal-induced sleepy dreams, one character got tangled up with another, roles changed, saviours turned into perverted criminals, so that one no longer knew who was who – nor did it seem to matter. Their chief task was to find a mountain pass where horses or elephants crossed, steal a horse at an opportune moment, escape this fraught history, and find a clean place to live. We won't move from here, plenty of timber in this forest, as soon as the house is up – and so as not to feel so lonely – we'll have Aunt Marcelina come and stay with us. Filling their lungs deep in the clear, damp morning air, they heard the dull roar of the sea – that's how close they were. Who was right, then? came the percussionist's sudden question, as he departed from his text in a different tone of voice, checking on whether they were following him. And once more his voice put things in their place. Horses stolen for a getaway went back to their stable or mountain pass, elephants to their pens, perverted criminals to prison, saviours on to their pedestals. Bye, bye, little cottage by the sea. It went up in smoke, a glow-worm's glow. Bye, bye, Aunt Marcelina, sorry to have caused you any trouble, such a long journey and all for nothing. And take care when he begins firing questions not to mix one character up with another but be sure to unscramble them and have everything fall into place. Remember, if you want to escape punishment, say 'the saviours' when it's the goodies' turn. Anyone caught napping and making a mistake had to spend the rest of the day under his or her bed, watching real little spiders scurry over the floorboards. These, however, were not half as terrifying as the spiders you imagined.

Memorising things was hard – concepts, the jargon of truth with no funny ideas upstairs. Luckily Nabu did not ask for dates or numbers, otherwise no one would have passed the long, long course in Percussionism. The Latin American population explosion was one of the few concepts that, by sheer repetition, he managed to drum into them more or less purely, but what the words and their nice rhythms meant completely escaped them. The figures had a certain cheery ring to them, something like a drum roll or a gallop, and the kids turned them into a plaything. In a game of hide-and-seek, instead of saying gotcha, gotcha, you're in the wardrobe, they'd scream with glee and say the Latin American Population Explosion. They felt they were putting a name to secret, mysterious things, a kind of melodious jewel that bedazzled them. Nothing less than LAtin AmErican PopulAtion ExplOsion. Explosion, indeed. What an unbelievable pleasure.

An expression that important deserved being translated into the new language in two versions, audio and silent, for use according to circumstances. It was important not for its meaning but for the use they made of it for naming Nabu, as if in not making any sense of the word they were returning it to him. With an abbreviated sign, then, they could say Nabu, saviour, and percussionist all at the same time, putting on the word whatever connotation they wanted. This also came in handy for saying, as a kind of shorthand, watch out, here he comes; he's looking this way; or, careful, here comes the Latin American Population Explosion.

The sermons gave rise to what Cholo called pointless evasions or impossible dreams. Yet when a dream was the only thing that the family could touch without feeling fear, that dream was no longer pointless. When the Aballays gave serious consideration to the possibility of transferring their real dreams to this other side, the whole thing became a matter of finding the adequate channel for making the transfer. When they found that whatever they were able to imagine belonged to them and that Nabu could not get at them there by tapping his baton and taking their photos away from them, Aunt Avelina could remain alongside the honeysuckle without worry. When the Aballays responded to a vital need – for you cannot stay alive without some sort of freedom – they had already invented their bird. Now they had to let it fly, let it come over to this side in some gap in the logic, seek the connection, the link between this house with its blacked-out windows and the little seaside cottage where they would invite Aunt Marcelina. There had to be a way, something that moves by stealth, a minnow that journeys from river to sea, stirring ancient magic as it makes its way between crevices in the rocks.

There were sermons on things that had no reality, sheer ghosts that vanished the moment Nabu finished reading, meaningless words left spinning round foolishly in the air, unable to take on any real shape, horses and cannon that after being together for so long merge into a single object, half iron, half hide, an imaginary animal and ugly to boot. There were sermons like the antics they were forced into to show their cheerfulness. Like the songs they were made to sing – to keep them from looking emaciated – about local people whom they invented and who had no relation to them, about clothes they invented, about words nobody used any more, old native ways as a substitute for silenced history. Tap-dancing.

Oh boy, Sunday again, said the kids (it was a Tuesday), seeing Nabu waltz in with his papers. The dog was now in a quieter state, drowsing on a chair and trying in vain to shut his missing eye. Be careful when Nabu starts asking questions, and don't mix up characters like that time when by mistake the saviours ended up in prison (and they under the bed). Quiet everyone, Nabu's got a boxful of scorpions.

'In yesterday's papers,' Nabu read, 'I read an interesting article on electronic psychiatry, which shall be the focus of my address today. To begin with, I'll explain the meaning and scope of the term, since this is probably the first time you will have heard of it.'

What they were going to hear for the first time, but by signs (as there was no other way round it), was Kico's account of his two or three meetings with Aunt Avelina's husband, hereafter referred to as 'the tourist' so as to circumvent potentially dangerous intrusions. By now Sila knew all about Cachimba, but Cholo and the others were still in the dark. Kico had anticipated his report during their meal, when he tapped the table with his fork – forks were once again permitted – and crossed his fingers. Try not to be alarmed, but I have to tell you I've been with Cachimba. The others' spoons froze on the spot, the fats and starches on their plates congealed. When Kico told them that Aunt Avelina was dead the spoons fell pensive. Tiny red spots on their backs, because their aunt was more alive than ever now. She had died in the honeysuckle but was still alive in railway stations, full front and profile (so you're hiding, so you're stealing from Uvelina?), fluttering about the house once more, a bird of ill omen, making knees go rubbery – a good thing the kids understood not one word of it. And the sermon mixing up their fears and hopes and Cachimba's words translated by Kico, obviously the other side, they now on the other side, everything happening now true according to Nabu's logic. In his wars, his conflagrations, his frozen heart, they were hearing all Nabu and Cachimba's craziness, everything blending into outbursts – how hard it is, trying to be free in the midst of the percussionist's iciness.

I'm talking now about a tight system of control over citizens, one presently applied in so-called civilised or industrialised countries, which dare criticise us, though you may be unaware of it, characterising our traditional way of life as a bloodthirsty dictatorship – yes, that's what they call it – and doing so in the name of certain human rights, which so far nobody seems to have defined. Pay close attention to what you're about to hear so you'll know what those countries that criticise us are like and by comparison draw your own conclusions and he was dressed up like a hunter, like those who use a blowgun *under this system of civilised people – and I say civilised between quotes – every citizen, without being aware of it, is subject to the automatic control of a serialised electronic computer* whatever the hell that may be but he never told me how Aunt Avelina died, though it's easy to imagine, watch out, he's about to turn round *in the hands of the central power, which is able to find out even what people think in a Machiavellian psychiatrisation of daily life* to keep in touch and said we'll be getting messages from the compadre, here, and we'll be free *and this way millions of telecomputer terminals spread up and down the face of these advanced countries* all of us free in the little cottage so Aunt Marcelina can come and live with us, find the opening among the rocks that connects the river and the sea, the tourist says they're building new jails and really it's a privilege to have a saviour in your own house, others are worse off *citizens are subject to rigorous police, medical, military, social, economic, religious, ideological, neurological, and sexual control, most of the time getting all the wrong data but they're the ones who speak of freedom, please bear that in mind* we're never returning to this house and meanwhile we'll live at Aunt Avelina's, she has lots of beehives and honey, she'll let us play in her garden and we'll eat black figs, of course I remember Aunt Avelina, whenever we went to her house she came out with a big plateful of black figs, how ugly that dog's empty eye socket is *these computers, programmed according to codes of behaviour drawn up by the central power of those countries, furnish technical data accurate to a high degree while they disregard the moral consequences of a percentage of citizens who, due to an insufficiency of computers, are daily victims of the uncontrollable risks of that blood-stained – yes, blood-stained – system of control avant la lettre, however much they speak of rights* but we have to find this out right away, the thing is I didn't want to scare you and, anyway, I never had the chance, he was always there sticking his nose in, it looks like they took Aunt Avelina away and asked where her husband was, the rest we know, and he'll say as soon as he finds out the whole story, he'll say I was expecting that, I knew she was in a viper's nest, I knew it from the start, I don't know why I didn't get on with things then, squashing the cockroaches in their own sewers, so they had none other than Cachimba hidden in the house, waiting to murder me by cutting my veins with razor blades, but very soon now all this will be taken care of *even the legal system has introduced this system – it drains the cup of sorrow – and laws have been replaced by so-called electronic jurisprudence* impossible dreams, how to get the percussionist out of here, we have nothing, but he spoke of God only knows what people and animals training in the hills, come on, that's crazy, and as soon as he finds out he'll say, just when you were about to get more freedom and better treatment you bring this up, mind you, I'm sorry but what I'm going to do with you now you'll never imagine, the spoon was the limit, first the spoon and now beyond all limits Cachimba, I put up with the spoon but this is the end, and right now you're going to tell me who the other aunts in the photographs are, the accused Céfira, accused Marcelina, accused Francisquita, all together, and the lot of you along with Cachimba will dig up their graves, gutless cockroaches along with Cachimba there in the grave, and he said soon we'd be getting messages from the compadre, for each family will have to take on its own saviour at the first chance, resorting to any means, fantasies, the raving of locked-up men *even the judges have been replaced by the computers' electronic memories, so that it is no longer man who judges man but a machine with an implacable will, and here one should ask what's better then, the mistake of one man or the mistake of a machine, which, not counting inevitable technical flaws, makes mistakes in most cases, since for the time being you can't speak of human ethics, even though they talk of freedom and justice* and when that day comes take the percussionist and then everyone else out into the street and let happen what happens, but that's nonsense, he'll know beforehand, he'll say, well, it's all over now, look where you are now, how low you have fallen, all because of Cachimba, Cachimba was over and done with this morning, we sent him to keep Aunt Avelina company, they're close together now, all of you, get into that lorry that's waiting for you, and you won't be seeing me any longer, my mission's over and Cachimba's dead, from now on you'll have to deal with other people, outside Hualacato, of course, no, you needn't take anything along, you'll need no clothes or papers, silent and orderly as ever get into that lorry, I'll seal up the house today and send ahead all your records, the final evidence that will reach its destiny well before you, they'll be waiting for you there, you'll remember me and long for bygone times, start practising your tap-dance, songs, and antics, activities much sought after at the place you're being sent to along with other cockroaches like yourselves, cockroaches together in the lorry with Cachimba's corpse, looking for a small spider, you'll all tap-dance in rhythm, for they are all percussion-ists there, I'm truly sorry, I did my best to save you, messages will arrive, a nice trap to immobilise him, then justice will be done, *thus destroying all individual freedom, which they purport to defend, even though they speak all along of freedom and rights, criticising us, but as can be clearly seen, risks resulting from the abuse of computer technology can come to destroy – as in fact is happening – freedom, justice, and the last human reserves, because no one so far can answer the key question – who controls computers? But they speak of rights. Now try honestly to compare your situation with that of the inhabitants of self-styled civilised countries and be happy you're still living in Hualacato.*

A sermon that was hard to memorise, they have not understood anything. Nabu's words, mixed up with Kico's report, were still buzzing in the air, fears and risks blend-ing, someone's sealed the rocks and the minnow can't find its way out. They go off to their rooms followed by wasps, with the word *Cachimba*, associated with wild animals, still filling their heads and making them weak in the knees.

10

NO RAISED VOICE, no muttering, nothing. The strength of the true percussionist came out now in his silence, the controlled sound of his technique, which, functioning on little more than a word or two, moved in a silence of unhappiness. He had kicked up a fuss about a spoon, screaming like a madman, issuing wild threats, and now, over this, nothing, a word or two and a mechanism of silence for locking up Cholo and Coca, separating and holding them incommunicado, night-time rules applying in broad daylight, the maximum penalty, for example, for tampering with a seal. Sila turned the matter over in her mind but could not make head or tail of what had happened, especially the part about Aunt Francisquita.

A percussionist switching from words to silence after a radio message had been received to say that at Aunt Francisquita's – a relative of the Aballays, it had been stressed – a photograph had turned up. By the serious look on the photographed man's face he could be none other than the much-wanted Cachimba. How coolly they were informed of this, how calmly Cholo and Coca were placed in solitary confinement and were now being interrogated in a back room, where Nabu kept so many things of which they were unaware.

Don't doze off, they'll be bringing you sandwiches, Sila told the kids, not noticing that the kids were already asleep, still in their clothes, lying across their cots, half-finished paper cut-outs in their hands, Julito's arm hanging over the side. There was a feeling that something had begun to break, hopelessly, and that they were trapped amongst the pieces. Sila put an ear to the wall again, then listened in the direction of the transom. Nothing. It seemed as if no one were home. No interrogation had ever been so silent.

Not particularly insistent, a percussionist asked Coca to tell everything she knew about her aunt, and Coca said her aunt was just those snapshots of a wedding, a handful of postcards, her aunt was more than anything a white wedding gown, the story of that gown after two long periods of mourning. How awful to remember now how Coca had put her hands over her ears to stop hearing Nabu refer to Aunt Francisquita as *the accused*. What could her aunt's saviour be doing to her now? Her aunt, dressed in white from head to toe – what were they doing to her behind the black pasteboard covering her windows?

Sila lay down on the bed again, in her own white dress, thinking about Aunt Francisquita as if she were thinking about herself. Auntie's been groped. If she has been, what'll happen to the rest of us? Aunt Francisquita does not belong to the everyday world, she's in her white gown after two long periods of mourning, she's no more than that, a gown and a party, the memory of some musical tops maybe and nothing else. So how could they possibly lay even a finger on her dress? Or on Uncle Carlos, who married her because he could barely see, otherwise who would have loved her after so many years of dyeing clothes, stirring black anilines into boiling vats out in the patio. After all that, any hand that touched her – however clean – would soil her white dress. If she's been groped, it's impossible to think she got married, that there was a party, that Céfira had sewn her gown (would they touch up Aunt Céfira too?), that they sliced the cake and left for the seaside the next day. It was all a pack of lies, then. If she's been interfered with, none of those things ever happened.

A percussionist who saved his breath by substituting facts for questions, which was more in keeping with his technique of silence. His question quoted the radio message. Look here, we've found a compromising photograph, the accused Francisquita with Cachimba. The accused is closely related to the Aballays, who are under suspicion. Investigate on your own and report back. Over. All saviours were in communication so as to soil Aunt Francisquita's dress, at night, when their apparatuses perform better. And then looking at photographs with Nabu, as if he were a family member and it was raining or too cold to go outside, who's this, yes, of course, this is Aunt Francisquita. And who are these, these, these, in a low voice, not shouting now, each of them telling him separately what he or she knew about their aunt, her brief history typewritten at length, so many hours for talking about no more than a dress and a party. Just a moment, he cut in, and he filled a page with two words they had spoken to him, as if he knew more than anyone else about their aunt. And his finger and the hairs on his hand pointing to another fact, without asking anything, without words, the finger pointing to a gap in the photographs. Between numbers 194 and 196, a snapshot was missing. How do you explain that?

If only he had shouted instead, all of you up against the wall looking for the little spider, as had happened with the spoon, a little shouting and nothing else – but no. Instead, a mechanical speed so that Coca sleeps alone in the sewing room; so that Cholo, directly responsible for everything as the head of the family, can have a good think about who stole the photograph. All breaks suspended for ever, of course, and all interrogations carried out silently in the back room. Leaping from transom to transom, scared out of her wits, Belinda was never present.

An extremely calm voice saying there's a thief in this house and I'll find out who it is, I'll also find out down to the last detail everything you're keeping back about this woman, and I'm going to communicate like the rest of you in that war language I know you've invented. Everything expressed so calmly, with gentle movements of his hands, fatality striking so quietly. Of course, after this you'll all be reclassified – but as something I prefer not to mention. It goes without saying that it's all over for you at the factory, that in general everything's coming to an end for the lot of you.

For Sila, however, Aunt Francisquita was the heart of the problem – or at least her aunt was at the heart of it. Having discovered their language, how far could Nabu get? It's something all prisoners do. How far, when the only thing he had against them were a few family snapshots. Their most serious crime was having stolen Aunt Avelina's picture. Yes, it's true, we were afraid, that's why we stole it; but it was our picture; we were afraid because we knew she was Cachimba's wife. Was it our fault she married him? That's their business. Right, punish us for stealing, then. But you can't take this any further than a couple of snapshots. They're dead images, memories. This isn't serious enough to warrant your saying everything's coming to an end for us. Look, all we have is a few photos, there's nothing else. Maybe he'd understand. But Aunt Francisquita had been groped, and this was what made matters worse. To speak of Aunt Francisquita in Hualacato was like speaking of a saint, such sweetness, her life barely came into contact with the world, as everybody knew, if you don't believe it ask around, phone anywhere and ask about her. But they had interfered with her, now she was the accused Francisca, Franchisca, Cachimba, cockroach. And if they had touched her up, there was nothing to be hoped for; if they had, Kico was on the fringes of contact with Cachimba, photos jumbled together, all of them in the pictures would die and not even the dead would escape.

She covered her ears with her hands so as not to hear her memories. The way she mixed things up was overdoing it. There was no reason why Tite should be involved in this. As soon as she drifted into sleep her mind began distorting things. She'd better stick to what was most immediate. But the immediate included the physical prolongation of her thoughts. Kico or Cholo or whoever was in the back room, answering precise questions that were becoming distorted in her mind, and everything as still as in a photograph. It was impossible to tell who entered the room with Nabu, impossible to tell how long they had been there. In her mind, in the photographs, four hours or fifteen minutes were all the same. And Belinda's green eyes still shining at the top of the transom, mixed up with Cachimba's messages, animals in the woods. Suddenly Belinda is a tiger coming down out of the woods, bringing madness.

II

THE PERCUSSIONIST SWEPT aside leads and apparatuses so that the old man's chair could squeeze into the room. Nabu drew the curtains, plunging them into complete darkness, and then lit a small lamp. Old Aballay stared wildly at the battery of devices. Nabu looked him straight in the eyes and asked if he was afraid.

'Yes, a little.'

'My question's quite simple. Who stole Cachimba's photograph – and why? You have five minutes to think it over. Remember, the others made a clean breast of it and did not descend into pointless lies. Their punishment will soon be revoked.'

Thinking was like searching the wall for a little spider. You focused on one spot, and everything else stood still. Because when you're looking for a tiny spider nothing moves. Disconnected words came to him, and from one moment to the next verbs no longer existed. Collecting his thoughts was impossible. The few words at his command were the direct opposite of those required. All he could do was to stare at the wall in search of the spider, which in this case was the percussionist's hands, working like the levers of a machine to open boxes and turn light switches on and off.

Precise, measured movements. Nabu's number one hand takes a sheet of paper from a box and places it on the copier. Hand number two turns on a light that projects an image on to the paper. The image disappears when the light is turned off, and the hand then takes the page away and dips it into a tray containing liquid. Meanwhile, hand number one takes another sheet of paper from the box and places it on the copier, then number two switches the light on again. Another image appears for a second or so, until hand number two makes it disappear by switching off the light. Number one sees to the page, dipping it into the liquid, while number two prods at the previous sheet with a pair of tongs and gradually, out of the swirling liquid, an old man's face emerges – his. He is winking and using sign language. The man in the photo, who is quite visible now, is saying a word whose meaning escapes old Aballay for the moment, while hand number one dips the second sheet into the liquid, which, once swirled round by number two, begins to reveal Cholo making similar gestures.

'Do you recognise yourself?' said Nabu, holding up the first photo with his number two hand.

'I've already told you we use these signs to while away the time. House arrest has been hard on us. We tell each other stories, share memories.'

'All right,' said the percussionist ritually, his numbers one and two perfectly still at last. 'For the time being let's leave aside this matter of war language and pass on to something more important. Let's talk about Cachimba. Come closer.'

As if he had forgotten something or were very tired, Nabu made his way to a wardrobe where, slowly, number one opened some boxes and, also slowly, number two rummaged among the metal objects it found there. The slow pace changed Nabu. His hands had grown and were now more important than the percussionist himself. When everything was in place inside the boxes, the hands turned to the old man. Like a rising cloud, numbers one and two cut off the horizon, blocking the old man's sight.

'I beg you,' he said as best he could, 'whatever you're going to do to me, do it fast.'

At this point in his story old Aballay did something akin to what was done in the films of a bygone era. When there were naked backs and a kiss and a bed, the light suddenly went out or the camera panned towards a large window where curtains ballooned in a breeze. Then, beyond the window, the camera would focus on a stretch of river shimmering in the moonlight. Depending on his mood, the old man resorted to one of two variations of this. Either he began talking about Eskimos or he recounted the plot of a film. He would say it was the intermission, with live acts, as in the past; somebody playing the piano, somebody else singing, after which we all went on happily watching the film.

In the film, which had a complicated plot, a medical student had to perform an emergency operation when he had never before as much as laid eyes on a scalpel. But the patient's life hung by a thread, and the would-be doctor had to pluck up his courage. To make matters worse, there was barely any light in the operating theatre, and the doctor's knowledge of human anatomy was equally dim. Not an easy plot, the old man used to say, but perfectly comprehensible if one called on history and zoology.

The Eskimo tale was simpler. An Eskimo grandfather leaves his igloo, barely wearing a stitch, and stands there by his home to be eaten by polar bears. The bears are hungry, for there is no food at the Pole. Luckily, there is a supply of old Eskimos, the polar bears say. But at this same time a baby Eskimo is born in the igloo, and in the struggle for survival there is not enough food to go round. Aware that he is one mouth too many, that he has lived long enough, and that others should be left to live out their lives, the Eskimo grandfather sheds his clothes in the igloo as though waving a goodbye handkerchief. To preserve his modesty he wears a loin cloth, which, since a dead man is ultimately a naked man, is unnecessary. May the cold kill me before the polar bears gather, thinks the old Eskimo, who fears the bears' hot tongues. In circumstances of this kind, whenever a polar bear approaches, an old Eskimo's heart wants to flee. It is an ancient custom of bears and Eskimos. The bears draw near, heads high, sniffing the wind, and when they catch the scent of old men who abandon their igloos (the animals know nothing of men's motives and are certainly unaware of a new little Eskimo's birth) they run, their teeth bared in the middle of the polar night, which, as everyone knows, lasts six months. The Eskimo grandfather sees the bear closing on him and he shuts his eyes, surrendering to custom. The bear will eat its fill and become heavy and will barely manage to lumber along over the snow or ice. At some point the other Eskimos will hear the bear. They know that after its meal of the old grandfather the bear is torpid and cannot defend itself. Then they take up the chase. Unable to run, the bear will be killed and the Eskimos will have food for many weeks. These are customs. The Eskimo baby will eat and grow strong with so much fat meat; he will learn to hunt bears, and he will have lots of clothes made for him from the skin of the bear that died because of custom.

In the film the doctor opens the door of the operating theatre, crosses the waiting room, and has to make way for visitors, who sit in chairs against the wall and begin knitting to while away the time. The doctor appears to have done his job well, in spite of his inexperience. Nothing could be worse for a surgeon than to lose a patient on the operating table. This is why he lets visitors in. They will be allowed to see the patient, but they must be very quiet, for the patient is still under anaesthesia and needs silence. The visitors have brought their children along, and they too knit, sitting on the floor, their backs to the wall. The doctor looks at them, hesitates for a moment, rubbing his nose, and sends them out of the waiting room. Kids will not be allowed to bother the patient. And at once the doctor appears, pushing the patient in his surgical chair.

It had had all the makings of a serious case – an emergency operation, rudimentary instruments. Pale, bloodless, a long, thin old man lay asleep, half dead, and his hands – which could not move on their own – swung with the motion of the chair. Watching the visitors, the doctor took the patient's pulse. The doctor had a crazy look on his face – his skin was almost red, he had a moustache and eyes that were unlike those of a person, a red face compared to the pale face of any patient recently operated on, a face crying out for a transfusion. All this was a cinematic device employed to tell the story, which often on the spur of the moment departs from logic – like what, for instance, the cat was doing at the hospital. From time to time the camera zoomed in on its eyes, a cat with a bow round its neck, lying up on a wardrobe, from where it stared at the man who had just undergone an operation.

The waiting room seemed more like a wake, with chairs lining the walls and the old man in the middle like a corpse. The doctor's fingers fly over the keyboard of a typewriter. A scalpel lying beside the machine begins to slide towards the edge of the table, helped along by the vibrations of the typewriter. It is about to fall when a quick movement of the doctor's hand replaces it by the machine as his fingers type on. The people in the chairs say nothing. They look down; they are knitting and they look at their work while waiting for the anaesthetic to wear off and for the old man to say something or at least to stir. The old man is lying on the surgical chair, which is folded out like a bed, his shirt is torn and his hand swings like a pendulum. Suddenly he takes a deep breath; the old man has at last moved; the sun is setting behind the Andes; a condor flies against the light; and everyone is knitting without uttering a word. The doctor finishes typing and stamps the pages with a seal. The cat looks at the doctor. The scalpel is motionless beside the typewriter.

The doctor has the visitors sign their names to one sheet, which he himself signs. Then he shakes the old man, waking him, sticks a pen in his hand, and the old man signs, opening his eyes as best he can. He comes to, scribbles his signature, and shuts his eyes again. He seems unaware that he has been operated on and is waiting for the anaesthetist again. Let it be over quickly, the old man thinks. The knitters look at him, their needles frozen in mid-air. A male nurse opens a barred door that leads on to a terrace, where it is growing dark. He gives the operating chair a shove, and the old man goes bouncing out and is lost among stones. The doctor bars the door again, and we no longer know whether we are in a hospital or a lunatic asylum. Everybody looks mad. The surgeon's red face has the blood the old man lacks. The doctor goes to his room, opens the window, and once more we see the old man outside in his chair, looking up and touching his face as if it were not his. He caresses it slowly with one hand and propels his chair with the other, escaping the surgeon's glance. The chair with the old man comes in through the rectangle of the window, trailing frayed ends. The old man vanishes off left, but the frayed ends of rags he drags behind – like the tail of a kite – can still be seen.

In the next scene the doctor or male nurse behaves strangely. He rummages in the old man's room, smashes the wardrobe with some tool or other, and takes the mattress off the bed. Ripping it open, he stands in the middle of the room looking for things, destroying, piling up old shoes, old clothes, objects and papers, everything. In the middle of the room a removal van, the walls are bare now and there are no chairs or shelves, piling things up on the floor, and the visitors knit in silence, biting their lips, in chairs against the walls like at a wake, everyone silent, the surgeon too, the only sound that of things being turned out and breaking and that of the closed window, which is hard to open, the window frame swollen tight, but it opens in a burst, and we can see the garden. There is the splintered window frame, a cabin trunk, a chest like a bursting insect. The cat with her bow comes flying through the window preceded by her own cry, and her untied bow streams down like a yellow thread. Then one sees the man is not really a surgeon, and he is angry about something he has done to the old man. It's hard to tell, one arrived after the film had started, and the doctor seems to hate the patient for something he has done. You begin to wonder, let's see, who's this, the sick man, and suddenly it's clear. Of course, the actor playing the surgeon is in fact the patient dressed up as a doctor to take revenge for something. The actual doctor may be the old man, and the knitters his assistants. The sick man took over the lunatic asylum, where he had formerly knitted like one of the patients, and now he retaliates by operating on his own doctor and keeping the doctor's assistants knitting. Knit, you bastards, the way I used to knit. It's fairly certain that in the reel we missed, in the operating theatre, the patient dressed up as a doctor laid the doctor on the operating chair and drained his blood. The patient then gave himself a transfusion of the doctor's blood and is now a doctor and a patient and has a dual personality. In one of them he smashes things and throws live cats out of the window; in the other he keeps visitors quiet.

At this point, I began to understand the plot. Whenever you come into a film late it's a matter of patience. Another trouble with this one is that it was silent. The soundtrack consisted solely of the noises of things being piled up and of the cry of a cat hurtling out of a window; the rest was silent, like the old films. The one clear thing was the wail of the cat, a human voice. Wailing cat is a figure of speech; it was probably the old man. Probably the effects of the anaesthetic had worn off, post-operative pain had set in, and the old man was wailing. You felt a bit sorry for the doctor, forced to play the role of an incurable patient waiting in the operating theatre while imagining the scalpel in the sick man's hands. But I'm healthy and don't care about the other guy, his gloved hands picking up the sterilised instruments. He has a tray full of them, but as he has no training he sticks the scalpel in anywhere, mistakenly, you know nothing about medicine, not there, please, those are vital organs, and now the effect of the drugs is wearing off and you hear the cat wailing with a human voice or the old man wailing with a cat's voice, it's hard to tell which.

After this scene things become clearer, you can follow the plot now, you can even figure out the film's title, *The Rebellion of the Sick*, or something like that, while the old man's last few belongings are thrown out of the window, they too guilty and punished as he is, things that always lived with the old man and so are also guilty. The old man, outdoors beside the pile, sees his life coming out of the window, the small objects of his life piling up at his feet, the ponchos, seeds, shawls, boxes, papers, medicines, hats, and the ignited scrap of paper that starts the fire. The old man sees the flames and looks back on his life, a rather corny scene, while the doctor or sick man goes on throwing things out – a blanket, a *charango* without its strings, a notebook for groceries bought on tick, a hackberry walking stick that is quick to burn, an earthenware jug, a mattress, a pipe, two pairs of trousers, a straw pallet, two pairs of long drawers, braces, two garters, a chamber-pot, certificates of good health, good conduct, and disability. Everything going up in smoke together. Thin strips of rawhide, a falcon's claw, a bottle of oil for rheumatism, an ounce of gold, a clay god, a small box of buttons, a tinder-box, an Inca plate, a bank-book, a reed pipe-stem, plans of farm land in litigation, a shoe box filled with useless objects, a piece of thread, a waistcoat, a flea, a twig, and a close-up of the old man's identity card growing blurred.

Cut to a meal, everyone but the old man who was operated on eating in silence. A girl makes a sign to the owner of the hospital, asking if she can take a bowl of soup to the man who has undergone the operation. The owner is generous; she leaves; the old man stares into the fire, warming his hands. By the light of the flames his face has a better colour, but his hands shake slightly as he takes the bowl. Then everyone but the old man goes to bed. He'll have to stay there, outdoors, until he can stand it. He has not eaten his soup; the bowl goes cold in his hands. He lifts it to his mouth, sips it, and in the firelight a vine leaf falls into the flames. Indoors, the lights go out, curfew is sounded, the old man naps. Cats, which will keep an eye on his post-operative slumber, appear on the white walls.

12

EVER SINCE THE OLD man decided to turn Cholo into a dictionary, making him learn their invented sign language by heart so that if the need arose he could be consulted, Cholo had fallen into the habit of looking at things as if they were there to be committed to memory. He studied events with the utmost deliberation, viewing them in slow motion almost. This worked with signs, once they were written down, but not for events, which lose themselves in time even before they are over. As a result, events were plodding affairs for Cholo, and occasionally he confused the new language with life itself and would recollect things that should have fallen into oblivion and forget others that it might have been useful to retain, just because he was unable to link them to his sign language. Yet by looking at events with an eye to recording them, he projected himself into the future and by so doing was bolstered by a healthy certainty of survival.

Lately he was so wrapped up in his words as to be not quite there. He kept trying to get to the bottom of something he had just witnessed (a person passing by, an object falling) as though it were a new sign to be memorised. After what had happened and the old man's banishment, the family ate in their rooms, there were no more indoor breaks, and they seldom saw one another except for the odd peep through a crack or when they queued up for the bathroom before bed. Lost in his words, Cholo saw Kico and the percussionist go to the room where the old man had been operated on, but Cholo was so busy trying to slow the event down to turn it into a sign for his dictionary that he felt nothing.

The small signs and notices that the percussionist had pinned to doors and walls or hung from the ceilings had to be committed to memory. One by one, Cholo did so, and he even memorised those that no longer existed, also recording the history of each, for their texts and locations were constantly changing. And if walls were moved when signs were changed, Cholo committed this to memory too. He could draw the floor plans of the different houses that the house became according to the whim of Nabu's little notices, which complied with strict rules of security and surveillance, off limits, neutral zone, strictly forbidden, danger, yesterday's free area now absolutely forbidden, for Nabu has decided to spend the night there, and the little sign announcing it amounts to a barrier stronger than a brick wall, just as the sealed doors are better than any lock, for the night-time rules contain nearly three pages of injunctions about breaking these seals, all of which Cholo has learned by heart as an appendix of Latin tags to his dictionary.

Now to make a sign for Coca's uplifted arm as she got ready for bed and the stirring of his desire. Nabu assigned turns, Cholo going to the bathroom and Coca entering her room, but at the door she held back for a moment or two, ignoring regulations, ignoring Nabu, and raised an arm to greet Cholo and to become the teenage Coca once more, greeting him from a distance and stirring his desire. His desire fixes her, freezes her with a hand slightly raised; he can see her from the approaching ship, he feels his body growing to get closer to her. Opening a way between Nabu's signs, he tries to remember her body scattered among the years, among the notices. When he leaves the bathroom she is already locked in her room, the door sealed, but Cholo has slowed her down and can still see her at the half-open door, raising her arm to identify herself among the throng on the wharf. She and her raised arm become sign language for a naked body and desire. From now on, to lift an arm slightly will be enough to say I love you or I want you.

When the percussionist sealed her door, Cholo went and peeped through a crack, in disobedience of another of Nabu's posted signs. This one was not especially strict. Cholo was waiting for Belinda to get down and begin freely traipsing about the house, the signal that Nabu had fallen sound asleep. It was well known by now that some hair of the cat's whiskers sensed Nabu's state of unconsciousness. Desire had wiped out the words Cholo memorised, including Nabu's notices and the regulations. The dictionary was but a single blank page with a drawing of Coca, her arm up, identifying herself on the wharf. Coca is not her face or voice or gestures now; she is a body and her body is the only possible face in the world. There are no landscapes, the earth lives only in bodies, in Coca's body, which is waiting for Cholo in his sign language. Coca a teenager again, lifting her arm before shutting her bedroom door, like the first time in a maize field with a damp bit of earth in her hair and on her back the imprint of tiny stones; and from then on Coca's body had been like a long journey, like those injections that make you taste eucalyptus at the back of your throat the moment they enter the bloodstream. Cholo tasted Coca's body in his mouth, and he swallowed it.

It's now a long time since Nabu turned off the lights and the curfew bell rang. Belinda has not put in her appearance, but Coca's body is there waiting for him. She lifts an arm in the maize. His desire has blotted out the latest notices, and Cholo breaks the seals, makes himself thin, becomes a dream in the dark, and, finding out he is a thief, he steals sugar and a table knife from the kitchen – presents for her. He and Coca will hide among the growing maize. On that occasion too they were being watched. People thought they were picking maize but they lay on the ground, nibbling each other and from time to time rustling the stalks to make the others believe they were walking down the rows. Cholo is entering a neutral zone, the notice is quite clear about it, and he is just a step away from a strictly forbidden area. Coca's in this area, to be stripped naked in the maize field, in bed, anywhere, these are tricks of possession. Cholo steps into forbidden territory, with a full erection, in rut, the cat is afraid of corners, Cholo smells the ripening ears and hears the percussionist's breathing.

Like an object gradually lit on a stage, Nabu begins to appear. He'll forgive me, the situation is understandable; he'll punish me, of course; he'll send me away to die with the old man or to a jail in the south or somewhere in the north to dig ditches and build prisons, highways, like so many others; but nothing worse, because, after all, wanting to be with her is understandable. In the middle of the room now, as tall as if glimpsed from below, Nabu's figure stands perfectly visible. Apart from stealing, you were going to kill me with this knife, weren't you? Cholo thought he heard from a Nabu who was too silent. He can use his blowgun without worrying about who his victim may be, he's said that time and time again. Anyone in the dark in a forbidden area is a target, prey, a partridge, a sitting duck. He'll send me to jail, that's understandable; the situation is self-explanatory; kept apart from her for so long, it's only natural that I should desire her, that I should want to make her the gift of a table knife so she can eat more decently. And a little sugar, that's understandable; besides, all I did was break a seal. I know that's forbidden, but Coca was in there. The percussionist stands in a cone of light, shoe buckles and eyes shining, almost everything on him shining except for the blowgun he has aimed at Cholo, who suddenly becomes a little boy. The boy off to a neighbour's, bearing a small parcel and saying, my mum's returning the sugar you lent her yesterday. He was returning something to Coca, that's all, but you changed the notices. This area hasn't been strictly forbidden for quite a while now; I'm sorry, please forgive me; besides, it's hard to remember all these notices, these different things, all the rules; put down your blowgun and let's talk it over; you have to be understanding once in a while.

The percussionist's cheeks puffed out like a trumpet player's as he blew through his blowgun. Cholo felt pain in the region of his abdomen, a spreading heat that wiped out the sign for Coca along with the first words of his dictionary. At once other kinds of heat – having no human notion of time, unfamiliar with time – changed the order of events for him. Nabu couldn't possibly be there, not under these circumstances, for he had only just got to the house, he was knocking at the door, and they were inside saying goodbye to one another, he was just arriving and saying good morning, I'm the percussionist, and they were about to stand against the wall searching for a little spider. Something failed, was not true. In fact, Cholo was now breaking the seals of his door to go about some important business, which now slipped his mind, something like making sure the cat was walking freely about the house, when his abdomen felt the heat and then he was carried to bed, for he was ill, was that it? Let me go, I'm all right, he said suddenly, remembering that what he was about to do was to go to bed with Coca. So, stealing then, were you? What do you mean stealing, when I'm kneeling here in bed? His knees should have been sinking into the mattress and they weren't; the wet tiles, that's where his knees were. Nabu was running after him in the rain, Cholo's shoes, his sex, his memory all got wet; Nabu caught up because Cholo was on his knees. So, running away, are you? He tried to walk to Nabu on his knees to explain everything. I was going to lie down with Coca for a little, just while she was fast asleep. We weren't going to do anything wrong, please believe me. Cholo thought he was going towards the percussionist to offer an explanation, but the different forms of heat took him back to his childhood. That's why he was such a little boy. He struggled, saying he was in bed ill, his knees, and he couldn't walk. Perhaps he should ask the old man for advice. He had only to pluck up courage to open the locked window and peep into the garden. The old man was down there under the leafless grapevine; it was the season of the year for pruning. The old man would tell him where he stood in time; after memorising so many signs for the dictionary Cholo had forgotten all about time, but the old man had always been a keen star-gazer and knew every inch of the Milky Way. Yes, he would do so at once. He already knew that opening any window was strictly forbidden and carried a stiff penalty. But if he had tampered with door seals, opening a window was a lesser offence. He took down the notice from the window, folded it, and threw it out into the rain. The rain would erase it, mixing letters with mud, and it would get lost down the road when the water flowing from the hills turned the streets into rivers. The window was nailed shut from the outside. Window panes shrouded in black pasteboard? *Crash*, like in comics. How marvellous to see this light in the shape of a cone shining down on the old man. He is not in his chair, he has both his legs, lots of buckles, and a blowgun. You know what? I've got lost. I was going to see Coca, my eyes blurred, the little notice changed places, and I got lost. We had to do things together, as you know. She was waiting for me, the maize was high, and other people's indiscreet glances wouldn't reach us there. Everyone thought we were picking ears of maize and we were nibbling each other. She was waiting for me, and I couldn't go; I was on an errand to return some sugar to the old woman across the street, and Coca couldn't understand why I was taking so long, what I was doing with the packet of sugar in the dark. I meant to put away the sugar and knife I was going to give her, so as to be free to get there, but I couldn't find any place to leave them. It was quite dark. I'll get rid of this then, but where? It was raining, I'd be punished if I threw away anything as scarce as sugar. Something was failing then, something was not true. And mind you, Nabu has nothing to do with this; when I was returning the sugar Nabu did not exist. I think I ate the sugar then, that's why my stomach got hot and began to ache. And to rain. Then I began running, and it was nice getting my bare feet wet in the rain, and besides I no longer had the sugar in my hand; I was free, I could calmly enter the room where Coca was waiting for me, naked, as you know, to nibble each other while others thought I was returning the old woman's sugar. I was in a hurry, Coca was waiting for me; if I didn't arrive on time she'd have to sail on a ship, farewell, it was awful to think of her being far away, so sad. She was waiting to look at me with her body, with other eyes, blind eyes but eyes you can touch, you know that. She has been leaving ever since we were separated; she's been turning young again, going backwards, having birthdays in reverse; she wanted to go back to the day she was born, and if she got there it would be the unmaking of her; she'd be over, unborn, gone, that's why I had to get there, so she wouldn't go back any more, so I could stop her at some point in time; if she could look at me with her body we'd finally be somewhere, and now I've got lost, I can't walk, I must have stepped on one of those broken bottles you find in the mud when it rains; all because I wouldn't let go of the sugar packet, or because I no longer had it, I can't remember; I'd eaten it, which was why my stomach hurt, I was getting lost, I am lost; with my injured foot I couldn't walk, and the rain was getting me dirty, I was on my knees, I couldn't get there, and she was leaving the wharf where she'd been waiting, lowering her arm and getting lost in the crowd. So, stealing, then? It's my own maize, I'm not stealing anything, but I wasn't in my maize patch, I was getting lost, after all this is my house but I wasn't at home, I was crossing an empty site to return some sugar to the old woman across the street. So, you're stealing sugar? Ask my neighbour, she can tell you. But my neighbour wasn't there, her home wasn't there either, it was raining on an empty site and that was all, Coca wasn't there either, it was raining in her bedroom, my stomach aches, I don't know where to put the packet of sugar, it's very dark and Coca's not waiting for me, she's coming down, she's blind, she's not there. And I'm not there either, I'm lost; I've forgotten the signs, they're lost, and you insisted I keep track of them. Try to remember what's in your head; that can't be lost, it belongs to everyone; remember that you're the book. I dropped the book in the rain; the letters ran off the pages. You'll have to repeat everything all over again, I can't remember what the words were for. I haven't stolen the book. I dropped it in the mud, and it was washed away by the rain. And now tell me where Coca is. You can't be with Coca now. It would do her a lot of harm to be beside a man like that, getting wet and muddy, getting mixed up with other strange things. Try to remember the words I told you and then go to sleep. Leave the sugar and the ears of maize and Coca for some other time. The neighbour won't be angry if we don't return her sugar today. Go to sleep, the saviour will soon be around with his torch. And if it's true that it's raining, you can tell him – and you won't be punished for it – that the window panes were shattered by thunder.

He fell asleep trying to remember his mental notes; he fell asleep afraid he'd forget everything for good.

Nabu touched Cholo's head with his foot and, seeing that he was not stirring, went to fetch a bucket, a dustpan, and a broom. He began sweeping meticulously. He swept up the sugar, the knife, and Cholo, put everything in the bucket, and took it out to the street, where he tipped it all into a plastic dustbin and waited for it to be collected.

13

AFTER THE BOWL OF soup on the first day of his banishment the old man was given no more to eat. He lived on vegetable scraps and on the prison food his family smuggled out to him. These meals, which they poked out through air ducts, came wrapped in paper birds, toads, or rabbits. Meanwhile, old Aballay was forever looking up at the sky, waiting for the compadre's carrier pigeons. At night he sheltered in the small outside room. When Nabu came round on inspection every two or three days, the old man would go limp, pretending he was starving to death. Sometimes Nabu came close and touched him with his foot or his blowgun to see if the old man was stiff. All this time old Aballay was extremely busy thinking about a couple of paper cut-outs of his own design, training his birds, and tapping on the walls to communicate with the others. Communication was poor lately; many signs had been forgotten, and they had no dictionary.

Two messages could not be decoded. The first was from the old man, requesting material for a pair of cut-outs; but no one indoors understood it, and several days were spent in an attempt to decipher it. The second came from them, trying to explain about Cholo. Every night the same story, an ear up to the wall listening to the same rhythmic taps, which the old man already knew by heart without under-standing what they meant and guessing that the last bit said 'we'll try again tomorrow'. It got nasty when they managed to agree on the word *death*, a sign they had forgotten or one they somehow did not want to under-stand. They had no word to answer the nervous *who, who,* that the old man tapped out every night. When the family invented their language, it had not occurred to any of them to make up names for themselves.

When the south wind began to blow the old man rejoiced, believing it would bring him something. Huala-cato's south wind blew once a year and shifted things from place to place. When it did, people living out in the country had to hold fast to trees so as not to be blown away, and they had to dodge wheelbarrows and sheets of zinc roofing that whirled round in the sky. This time it did not blow so hard – nothing like when it picked up Aunt Céfira's sewing machine, which had been left out in the patio, broke the wire fence at the back, and landed in the middle of Don Floro's house. Only light things were carried off now, a pair of trousers and other items torn from clothes lines, pieces of cardboard and lots of paper. The heaviest was a scarecrow. The old man could have used the trousers but they flew too high overhead. The wind was dying when a gust dropped a dead cat on the chicken-coop roof. Shirts and handkerchiefs passed almost within reach; he grabbed at them but they slipped past, and all he laid hands on was a woman's stocking. The next day, Kico saw a bird near the roof by the opening of his air duct. The creature was looking down, as if stunned. A thread from a woman's stocking was tied to one of the bird's legs; at the end of the thread was a slip of paper asking *who* in the old man's hand. *Cholo*, Kico wrote on the back and, careful not to snare the bird in the thread, helped it through the duct.

To take his mind off Cholo's death the old man concentrated on a series of new cut-outs that he had thought up. Little brother, I'm sorry but I need your skin, he told the cat brought by the wind, and he hung it from the peach tree to prepare it. It was a young, thin, calico cat, which had been lifted off a roof as if it were a feather. Cholo's death provided the old man with a direct connection to the mystery, forcing him to look at each thing as he tried to decipher it. He found that in the whole world there was no object or physical motion that was not at the same time a meaningful sign, like the ones they had invented. The problem was not knowing what they meant, just as he did not know what the ants that were beginning to eat the cat meant, what the saw blade in his hands that was removing the skin from the cat's flesh meant, or the stones in the walls of the house, or the cat's body buried near the gate, the sea, the Milky Way, the sun drying the cat's skin, the glint of mica at the tip of a stone, signs in the air, naked words that hid nothing, a perfect language that had no dictionary. When the skin was ready for working he shed these concerns and threw himself into the construction of his pair of cut-outs.

Looking at the stones in the walls of the house, he delved deeply into the question. Perceptions suddenly came to him in the midst of bewilderment, something meant to be said but that he could not manage to hear, the end of a cut thread. He could guess the weight of each stone, the shape of the face hidden in the wall, the empty spaces between one stone and the next. I have discovered what thinking is, he marvelled one night. In my own way, but it's thinking. Life's last gift amid so much privation.

The notion of repetition as a hidden sign worth studying came to him while he was reconstructing the time they were constructing the house. Day in and day out, Coca carried stones in the wheelbarrow from the gate, Cholo mixed mortar, Kico handed the old man bucketfuls of it, he set the stones one on the other and used the plumb line, Tite ran about getting lime all over himself. In other words, all summer long and a good part of the autumn, stones were shifted from one place and laid in another, until they reached roof level. Not only was the family building a house – which was quite a normal activity – but they were changing space by adding volume to it. This took on a certain importance if you appended to it the parallel observation of the bird that turned up at the same time at the same spot, every day, flying down from the same branch, crossing the same bit of ground by the same route, and absent-mindedly eating. It was pointless scattering seed anywhere close to its path; it didn't see it or, rather, refused it. Nor did it ever come near the little room at the back, where seed could always be found on the ground. And the bird flew off from the very same spot, always in the same direction, always over the fig tree. Their tasks were identical every day, and this made sense. The family laid stone upon stone repeatedly. The difference was that the bird changed nothing around it, and that too made sense.

One of their projected walls stood in the bird's path, but they had no intention of altering their plans for a bird, so they went ahead and dug the footing. The next day, pecking absent-mindedly at the edge of the trench, the bird looked down into it with some curiosity, hopped over it, and went about its business. They must have laid ten courses of stone, almost half the wall's height, when they noticed the bird behaving uneasily. The creature seemed hesitant, looking for a way round the obstacle before it finally flew over it. The old man thought about it for one whole night and made up his mind. Cholo did not like it one little bit when he saw the wall pulled down and the stones scattered on the ground. It was meant to be Tite's room, said Coca sadly. Kico cried; he had laid some of the stones himself. You had no right; it's just your superstitiousness, Cholo said. Tearing down the kids' room over a silly thing like that, and all our work down the drain. Luckily the bird had no problems with the new wall they put up. Otherwise old Aballay might have even pulled down the kitchen.

By then his intuition told him that birds were like tiny cosmic watches that weren't meant to measure time. They were time – or part of it. Their behaviour followed precise patterns, their migrations were equally precise. The whole of space was contained in their little heads, and they were thoroughly familiar with the world. Before the advent of humankind and of its ownership of the earth and air, unthinking but also unafraid, birds conceived the world as a great pleasure and divided it into happy plots and laid down their routes with that alone in mind, without either violating the planet or adding anything to it. Why cut an age-old route with a wall? Old Aballay had noticed that birds gathered in a certain tree every morning, chirped away for a good while, and then lit out in different directions, each to its territory, which it marked out by song, a word, and within which the bird had its own paths, its food, its games and festivals, its loves and nests. If they let us build this house on a plot of land that was always theirs, the old man said by way of justifying his actions, we've no right to interfere with the patterns they have followed since time immemorial, which is a long, long time, as I see it. That's superstition, Cholo said; they can sing anywhere. And he pondered that, the song of birds. To us they were songs, but weren't they signs? I think, the old man told Cholo without looking at him, that birds don't sing. What they do is a form of expression; it's a habit. I wish they could sing. With their voices you can't tell how birds would sing if they could sing. To say they sing is to deny them their language, which is an important part of their life. Birds don't sing, they live, they tell their truth. Maybe so, but they don't know it, said Coca, taking Tite away. They were slaking lime, and it was dangerous.

I knew it at the time, the old man told himself, staring at a particular stone in the wall and remembering its weight. I knew it but never developed the idea. When Tite died many things fell apart, and for too long we were like sleep-walkers. That's why, if you alter a bird's course, the old man said now, addressing Cholo as if he were alive, you're altering time, which, as everyone knows, is sacred. Birds never had to figure out the earth's roundness. It was round there in their heads and before their eyes in their flight. If we'd gone on with our wall, we would have altered a rhythm, a piece of time, even if they flew over the obstacle. To put it more directly, when you see a bird on the roof of a house or a jail, that bird is not there to visit anyone. It's there because the ground on which the building stands was part of its old, old path, where it found its seeds and insects, and if things go on like this we'll take their space away from them for ever, we will have violated time, and then strange things might happen. By their space is meant the eggs the female will lay so that there will always be birds, which, as with every living thing, are an extension of ourselves, and neither we nor those parts of us can disappear or else the world would no longer exist. Besides, houses and jails are depriving birds of their happiness, which is the bird's whole object – as it should be for us too. After all, are we not an extension or a part of them? The reason for their paths, the shape of their space, is still a mystery to me. Now that I've discovered thinking, some day I may find the answers.

The contemplation of these things made the old man nervous and forced him to move about to try to get over the upset his discoveries produced in him. In search of someone to speak to, he propelled his wheelchair from one of the garden walls to the other. This activity kept him from thinking normally. Up to now his cut-outs had helped him relax, but he had finished them. They were two kinds of small leather toads with articulated mouths for swallowing insects, and he hid his creations down at the sides of his chair.

He was upset, knowing he had little time left. There was no question that in denying him food Nabu had cast the old man out to die, but he could not go on pretending that he was dying for the rest of his days. Hunger has clear limits, and the percussionist had a blowgun – which is to say a rifle. Before the old man reached the limits of starvation, the only way to save himself was to discover the unknown shapes he knew had to exist. Old Aballay believed that if he found these forms he could prevent deaths and other kinds of violence, and this would be a truth to put an end to all the world's executioners. Their books that had been burned contained pictures of scientists who had saved lives by the discovery of microbes. He was doing the same, and now he had to come up with a way of finding out who the percussionist was, who percussionists were, what they were like inside, and what they were here for. Obviously it was not easy to study Nabu under present circumstances. He was armed, but his behaviour, his madness, his cruelty could be explained if the old man could unravel the mystery of the shapes. Once these were discovered, the percussionists would simply vanish, thereby saving many lives.

Birds did not come unless they were called from one place and one alone, a single point on that surface whose shape and extent the old man was looking for. It had been the same for the bird that made them change the plan of their house. Proof of this was the repetitive behaviour over the years of identical birds in order not to lose that original path. Old Aballay knew by experience that the intensity with which he could communicate with birds within a specified area depended on where he stood. If he were on the edge of the area, the birds came, reluctantly, not daring to approach, and they never took food from the palm of his hand. They looked him over, got scared, and flew off. If he were outside the area his calls were totally unheeded, and the birds simply fled from him. But they came of their own accord – always a bit wary, of course – if he happened to be anywhere near the central point of the area. Who knew what might happen if he hit on the exact spot.

Naively believing that the area's shape might be that of a circle, he drove a stake into the ground and, with a line and small stick, traced its outline. No bird responded when called from any point on the circumference, so he tested various locations within the circle itself. He imagined he was watching himself from the rooftop, and he saw a potty old man going round and round in his wheelchair within the bounds of the big circle, frightening birds off. He was a scarecrow that from one moment to the next might be blown away by the wind. The boldest birds did venture up to him inside the circle, and they even perched on his chair. But then they would almost immediately stop listening to him and scurry away in fright. It was plain that the necessary shape was an odd one, a shape unanticipated by geometry.

By this he found out that the meandering boundary of the area in question extended outside the perimeter of their garden. Only the birds knew where the line ran. How was he to find the centre of a figure if he had no idea of its perimeter, which, to make matters worse, was cut by walls, overhead cables, jails, operating theatres, graveyards, hunters, saviours, invisible masters, and huge ant hills? Maybe the centre was in one of the many jails built to lock men up in punishment for dreaming of a world without jails.

The birds' centre. He thought about it night and day, searching for it in the real world, in dreams, in childhood, in constellations, in what he could not see, in the future. I should never have thought of it as a circle; I've lost a lot of time following that line, he thought, staring at a fixed point in space where by then Achernar should be appearing. Surely in one of the many shapes of the constellations was the shape he was looking for. The idea of the circle came from his boyhood on the side of a hill, where potatoes and maize were grown. He and his father were out sowing when they saw it. It was a ring of reddish stones with a white one in the middle, undisturbed for centuries. The land was good there, and he went inside the circle to plough. Not in the ring, his father said without explanation, but that night, while they were eating, the boy was told briefly that that land was sacred and could not be touched.

The circle stood out even when the maize was tall, and the ring was there for years and years, until stones became scarce and were taken away to build prisons. The memory of the ancient belief made the old man think of another, and without touching the wheels of his chair but only turning its gears he positioned himself to see the whole Milky Way, the path of the dead, along which Cholo would now be journeying, making fun of everything.

How wonderful was the day he began to work out the figure's perimeter. A real festival, dancing solo in his chair within the walled garden, dancing with imaginary fireworks going off overhead. He had discovered nothing less than that each bird, after pecking its way along the ground, had a particular spot from which it flew off. His search for the shape fixed by the centuries was nearly complete. To find it, to locate its centre, he had only to connect the points from which each bird took off. This was proved by the fact that when he called them from the perimeter, which was just revealing itself, the birds looked hesitantly at him and in the end failed to respond. In a week of taking measurements, he found that the line of the perimeter came in and out of the garden several times. If the shape was closed at some place he had visual access to, the figure would be complete, and from there to its centre was but one final step. The toothed gear hidden deep in his chair allowed him to raise his seat enough so that if he craned his neck over the broken glass embedded in the walls he could pinpoint the spots from which the birds took off on the other side. He went on taking measurements until the last rays of the sun disappeared. A day or two more and he'd have the answer. The joy of it made him shiver. He shivered, in the middle of the garden, he and his chair shivered and creaked under the eyes of a gang of bored cats.

As soon as he reached the centre, he himself would be like the birds and would be in the world in a brand-new way. More than anything, he'd be able to tell everyone about it; wresting from the world one of its mysteries, he'd write a dictionary using fresh symbols. He would then go another step and search for the centre of humankind. He had also observed that birds never died a natural death within the space of the figure he was in the process of discovering. Any time they were found dead it was always outside the boundaries. They had a place to die, which was

why they could not change their paths, and they knew
which places were for life and which for death. Or maybe
they died when in an oblivious moment they left their
space. Otherwise, what can a bird die of before its time?
Men ate each other, killed each other, were masters or
slaves because they had not created – had not discovered –
a space in which they could live. Instead, they lived in the
place for dying, and herein lay the secret of everything –
of the percussionist, of jails, of violence, of torture, of
adversity. If the old man found out what made birds tick
he'd find out what made the world tick, and he'd locate
the centre of mankind. The percussionist would weep with
remorse. My goodness, how did I not see all this before?
Nabu will say. And I'll say, brother, I forgive you. Which
is why I must discover the centre before Nabu kills me. A
few days ago he touched me with his foot and said, what,
this one still alive? I'll have to refuse the food that drops
out of the air ducts. Once I locate the centre I'll be able to
gather everyone and tell them that if birds can have a centre
so can mankind. For old Aballay to be able to travel about
the world in his wheelchair tracing out the shape of the
figure in order to go on living – that was the truth. There
was no other reply to madness; he stood on the threshold
of holding in his hands the medicine to cure adversity.
Following Nabu's lead, the old man would post signs
round the figure's perimeter. Here ends the place for living
and begins the place for dying. Please do not enter.

At long last the compadre's carrier pigeons arrived. The
information they brought was confusing, repetitive, and
badly expressed. Writing was not the compadre's strong
point. Things are getting worse, you will soon receive
instructions, Hualacato is a disaster, the messages read.
Nothing new there. The old man had only to watch
Belinda up on the weathercock at night to know all that.

Belinda's tail twitched when she saw lights going on and off and dogs frantically pacing up and down outside the garden walls. Meanwhile, he had the first hint that the birds were getting ready to migrate. Each day their short, sharp cries grew longer as they tried to bring their calls together into one duration and rhythm. Once that was achieved – and it would not take long – they would leave for the other side of the world. If he had not pinpointed the exact shape of the figure by then, he'd have to wait another year to find its centre. In one year the percussionists would kill several thousand Cholos. The last message brought by the bird with the thread tied round its leg said that they had not seen each other for a long time, that food was becoming scarcer by the day, that the kids were taking on old people's habits, that they were short on protein, and that Kico had recovered from his emergency operation. And carrier pigeons kept announcing an imminent start, which never took place. They were to overpower the percussionist the moment they got a package containing blue balloons, which they were to send up from the roof when the operation was completed. That would tip off the Cachimbas as to what awaited them out on the street. Now and again packages that promised to hold balloons were thrown into the garden, but they contained chocolate, or oil for rheumatism, or coded messages for which the old man did not have the key. One day he picked up a package so light he assumed it to be packed with the blue balloons. It turned out to be a piece of blood-stained cloth – hopefully the blood was not that of anyone who 'had had to be having what had been'.

Old Aballay's pensive bouts of insomnia in the little room at the back were interrupted on a couple of occasions by the percussionist's prowling around in the wee hours in search of wailing cats. They had barely launched into their shrieks when a thunder from indoors met an explosion of cries and paws. Lightning bolts lay in wait for the thunder as the little cats fired radially, forgetting the garden's vulnerable walls. Divided into groups and covering overhead space that came within range of flares and hand grenades, the cats used other points in the air to hide themselves. The moment one group at one end went silent, at the opposite end the next would start caterwauling. Following the technique of crickets, the felines fell silent any time a flare went off or a torch was turned on. If a grenade exploded, their interrupted cry was taken up elsewhere. Nabu blew his top, fell apart, lost his dignity, turned wild. Still, this was his human side, the side that did not measure his words or act on mechanical laws but shouted like a man insulting cats. His insults were improbably beautiful, and they gave the old man unexpected joy as he pretended to be a scarecrow so as to escape the blowgun.

Achernar shone bright in the northeastern sky that night, but instead of looking at it the old man kept poking the little fire he'd lit to keep himself warm. Stirring the fire was a way of ruminating, of rescuing forgotten signs, of thinking about Sila. He had seen her that afternoon from his phoney bowing and scraping position, about to be turned into manure for the soil, when the percussionist followed her as she went looking for something in the little room. A gloomy Sila, going mouldy from all this pointless waiting around, on the margins of widowhood without ever having loved anyone, wrapped in a dress that was once white but that had been touched up in the same way that Aunt Francisquita's had; Sila, what passed for Sila, becoming mixed up with the signs the old man was looking for in the fire he stirred so as to find a way of saving her.

He heard the package come over the wall at the bottom

of the garden but went on poking the fire in spite of his concerns. The town was still captive, the time that dragged by still belonged to the percussionist, and he could very well appear just as the old man was picking up the parcel. Meanwhile, he was better off staring at the constellations. One of them might provide a clue to the ultimate outline of the half-figure he was plotting from the birds' take-off points. It was hard to concentrate, the parcel seemed to have a life of its own, and there was a strange ring round the moon. When the faint light that filtered through the air ducts disappeared he glued an ear to Kico's wall and he tapped out a message to say he was waiting.

While he waited he reconstructed his shape yet again. The take-off points he'd jotted down that day reached as far as Don Floro's fence, the farthest the old man could see over the jagged glass at the top of the garden wall. As the figure's perimeter seemed to be closing, the points simply had to run back into the Aballays' garden. This gave him nearly as much time as the birds had; when they set off he would be completing his figure.

Swelling with drivel, the ear held up to the stone and already gone cold was filled with Kico's tapping, which reported that Belinda had sniffed Nabu in the soundest of sleeps. So exaggeratedly violent was the old man's push that his wheels spun round. Sending off sparks, raising dust, the chair went straight for the garden wall and the parcel. All this wrapping, all this string round and round – and what for? But oh my goodness, my goodness, they're balloons. The Cachimbas have begun their journey.

14

HEARING A *tap*, *tap*, *tap* on the wall, Kico stared at the air duct. At first the sound was like that of a cane brushing the stones, something climbing up with difficulty, then like cardboard being crumpled. Standing on the headboard of his bed, his eyes nearly level with the duct, Kico saw before him the stealthy mouth of a small leather toad, followed by a second, identical creature. The pair of calico toadlets crept forward in the duct, prodded by a cane rod. Kico stuffed them into a pocket.

Preparing for a journey is not easy. So many things to bear in mind, especially if it's a long trip. Checking schedules, don't forget anything, weather conditions, roads. For birds it's even more difficult. Their numbers are vast, and they have to reach some sort of agreement. Generally there are at least three different outlooks, three different groups, each roosting in its own tree. Some have not fattened up enough to endure such a long journey, so let them take up places at the rear. But wait a minute, what I think is, the winds, the storms, and then there's the memory of catastrophes, unforeseen gales, cold rains, hailstorms, and many birds are stuck halfway in the flight – all risks to be run. The old man has touched them; they're hot, they're running a temperature. Each treeful has a rhythm of its own. *Ta ta*s prevail over *te te*s, and from the shyest comes a confused *ti ti*. Last-minute negotiations via fast shuttle flights are carried out amongst the three trees – ambassadors, pacts, the *ti ti*s throw in with the *ta ta*s, linking rhythms and trees. The *te te*s are still arguing, but it's a certainty they'll come round.

Taking over a saviour is no easy thing either. He's close to a god and so strong it's hard to admit he's not part of nature, of fate itself. What's more, thinks the old man as he taps on Coca and Sila's walls, there's always the possibility of failure. Belinda, the paper cut-outs – anything can fail. What do we know about warfare? Then there are all the unpredictables, such as a hurricane-like percussionist, his hailstorms, his verbs. Our system of communications may break down.

With an ear to Kico's wall, old Aballay imagines he hears something. Afraid? Yes, a bit, like the other time. So, making up codes, were you? No, that's not it at all. Nabu is sleeping soundly; Belinda's never wrong. These are balloons, then, are they? Nabu holds the old man's cut-outs in his hands. In extreme situations, commend yourself to your god, comes his father's voice, sowing on the hillside. But god belongs to Nabu and seems to be part of his vast holdings. The old man feels he has no god. And in these circumstances the gods of Hualacato are just too naive. Woodland gods, harvest gods, they haven't the voice of thunder or storm; they don't dress well either, snow and mud scare them silly, and men frighten them. They never come close but stay in hiding. The old man's afraid too, of course. Yes, a bit; everything's so difficult and with no god. And still no news from Kico.

Instead, three of the compadre's pigeons fly in like scared, crazy little fly-catchers. Repeated instructions yet again. Of course I have the balloons; of course we'll try.

Damn it, now it's a question of seizing him, and that's the hard part. Compadre, you'd better keep the pigeons for some other time. Of course we'll take him alive; we're not killers. I don't want to see your pigeons for a good long while; and there go the pigeons back home to the coffee-man compadre.

In an orderly fashion, as if entering a theatre and occupying all the seats one by one and in silence, the cats spread out along the garden walls. They are many more than usual. A double row of heads, separated by multi-coloured broken glass, rings the garden. With an ear to the stone and as if turning to the rhythm he has tapped into, the old man thinks that if the cats were to let out a howl they'd have one very crazy percussionist on their hands, a sad night of felines and a scarecrow in the Milky Way, resting alongside Cholo and waiting for Kico. But the little cats are sensible. Old Aballay sees them sitting on their paws, absolutely quiet, turning to their own rhythm.

The birds are still not in full agreement. It seems that the *ti ti*s will not give in, and the *te te*s say that if the mass of the *ti ti*s do not join the others, the *ta ta*s will end up on their own, since the *te te*s will fly back to their tree until things are cleared up. Emissaries shuttle back and forth to the dissident *ti ti*s' tree, setting up a true aerial bridge, while the *ti ti*s complain that they disagree with the set-up, that they cannot listen to the *ta ta*s and the *te te*s at the same time, and that each must come to them one at a time or, they say, we'll go mad. To top it off, the most uppity *ta ta*s are about to pull out of the assembly, fly to another tree, and declare themselves *to to*s. That's nothing, the old man thinks, in previous years it took them a lot longer to become *to to*s. And we have yet to see the appearance of a group of *tu tu*s; there will never be any agreement until all five vowels are gone through.

No, things have to be running smoothly there indoors, because everything is in rhythm – the cats on the walls, the birds about to set off, stars vanishing, and the house in its silence. He has no god and is dependent on a couple of cut-outs, and that's in rhythm too. He knows that rhythms bring things; when something falls into rhythm a chain reaction is unleashed, and that's why they'll be freed. It's an inner movement that brings it and that attracts things, thought the old man, changing over to his other ear and looking towards the wall at the bottom of the garden and the house next door, where a man had climbed on to the roof and was tying a balloon to the chimney. A minnow had just found the crevice amongst the stones and was swimming freely in the sea.

Sila and Coca broke the seals on their doors and peered out, facing Kico, who was approaching Nabu with a cut-out in each hand. In fact, what they had broken was their fear, and, all unawares, they were falling into the rhythm that had come into the house along with the cut-outs. The three looked at one another like strangers. I was dying to see you, how you've changed, the sort of thing people say to each other. Kico signalled to Sila to send the cat. When he saw Belinda padding nonchalantly past the percussionist, he tossed one of the cut-outs to Sila and pointed to the saviour's feet. The toadlets were automatic, and they closed perfectly round the percussionist's feet and wrists. None of them spoke a word as they watched the cut-outs firmly tighten. Outdoors the last few stars were fading in the sky, prisoners dreamed in their cells, jailers strolled up and down swinging their key-rings, tigers dozed, viruses stirred, ships burst with riches, insects slept with children, old men turned to their memories, young men turned back, houses sagged and leaned, streets were closed, graveyards advanced upon the desert and waters, the sea buzzed with indifference, in the mountains vicuñas understood nothing as they heard ice melting and stones falling, and out of their entranceways streamed the Cachimbas.

'Call the old man,' Kico said. He looked at the percussionist, feeling that he did not hate him, that he had gone beyond that, and that Nabu seemed to him more a machine that had broken down than a manacled man.

The women were just able to see the last cats withdraw, for the sun was rising. Listening with his right ear and looking towards the gate, the old man could not see them.

'Grandad,' Coca called.

They had to get him home by pushing his chair for him. Old Aballay had grown steadily weaker and could neither speak nor make any signs. He dried his eyes and in the end managed to tell them that his missing leg ached, which was why he had been unable to drive the wheelchair.

'Wonderful little toads!' Sila said.

'It was a nice cat, but its skin wasn't much good. I had to plait it,' the old man said, recovering the rhythm. He sat there staring at Kico, at Cholo. With his white hair and those scars, the two were identical. Kico laughed.

'I'm Kico, Grandad. I was left looking like this after the operation. You can call me Cholo if you want to. Let's see those balloons.'

'Good, home again,' the old man said, taking a quick look at Nabu and heading for the kitchen in his chair.

The others followed him, and the children tagged along too. Moderately starving at first and reasonably hungry later on, they ate up everything in sight.

'What's going on? Is the little drunkard leaving already?' said one of the kids.

Nobody answered. Without looking at one another,

they chewed in silence, directing a feline concentration on their meal. Grabbing hands reached for food none of them had tasted for a long, long time.

'I used to imagine this moment once in a while – but differently. It was always unexpected – embraces, laughter, tears. I never thought of it with a meal,' Coca said.

No one even bothered to remark. The one-eyed dog appeared in the doorway, growling at the unusual sight, but he would not drop the plastic bone the percussionist had given him.

'Shut up or there'll be a cut-out for you too,' the old man said, feeding the dog half a sausage.

'OK, let's see it,' said Kico. He handed the wine bottle to old Aballay.

The nails had been removed from all the windows so that they now opened. Fresh air poured into the house as a sudden black smell poured out through the skylight and chimney.

'Look! We're changing colour!' said the kids.

The lot of them were in a semi-circle round Nabu, staring at him. The old man took off his hat. His hair was full of twigs, leaves, and bird feathers.

'The first time I saw the sea, people still went around on horseback,' he said. 'I kept delaying my arrival from the very start of my journey. I wanted to let it sink in; seeing the sea for the first time is very important. I asked about it, and when I was told it wasn't many more miles I stopped to rest and smoked a cigarette, thinking how nice it was going to be to get there and what a short distance it was now. When the sea was within sight I stopped to look at it from a long way off. Then I began to hear it. We entered the waves a bit at a time, a bit at a time. The horse got its hooves wet and neighed with the utter joy of it; I let the water wet me by inches, any way it liked. It's a lot like that now, here with the saviour, but I can't really explain it.'

The percussionist opened his eyes. The first thing to reach his senses was the strong rawhide smell of the cut-outs that bound him.

'What's the meaning of this?' he shouted.

'A couple of cut-outs,' Kico said.

'This is the worst form of suicide you could have chosen for yourselves,' said Nabu. 'Not even a memory of you will be left. From this spot, without even moving, I can release viruses and microbes that will unleash an epidemic. So get back to your rooms, all of you, and send the old man back to the garden. Bear in mind that I could have killed you; as for Cholo, what happened was in self-defence. For the rest of you, we'll reconsider the problem before it's too late. As long as you obey me, I'll put my viruses aside for now. You do realise that a desperate act will get you nowhere. That's how I'll put it down in my report – so your punishment will be lighter. By now my superiors will have been informed of everything, and it won't be long before they release me and visit justice on you lot. So let me out of here at once.' This last he shouted in the same voice he had used when talking about the spoon.

'So what do we do with the little drunkard now?' said one of the kids.

'Well, we could start his trial while we wait for the compadre's instructions,' said Kico.

'I don't know anything about conducting a trial,' the old man said. 'Have the balloons been launched?'

A nearby explosion shook the house, and the shattered window panes became hailstones. Kico ran out.

'What you're attempting is madness,' Nabu shouted, outdoing the spoon. 'There'll be polio, whooping cough, yellow fever, black plague, summer diarrhoea, Chagas' disease, permanent blindness, and Parkinson's disease. We'll go back and raise the dead to kill them all over again.'

'What a show – almost the whole town full of balloons! And that was no bomb. Bricklayers and stonemasons burst out of jail using their own bodies.'

'I understand your attitude,' Nabu said in a low voice, collecting himself, 'but I can't condone it. In your place I'd have behaved the same way. You would be well advised to give up, however. We have all the weapons. Besides, I want to tell you that I have been obeying orders. I'm not the one who has mistreated you. After all, I'm from Hualacato too.'

'Once and for all, shut up,' said the old man, his ears pricking to catch new explosions.

'No, you lot shut up – infirm imbeciles; ignorant louts; thieves; beardless pariahs; bastards; faggots; pretentious, utopian, Goya-like protozoans; iconoclasts; felines; half-breeds; sons of a fucked-up whore.'

'Must he go on talking? He's gone mad,' said Sila.

'No, he mustn't,' the old man said. 'But give me time to think.'

Kico taped Nabu's mouth with a sticking plaster he'd been carrying in his hand. Behind the plaster, Nabu continued shouting.

The old man went back out into the garden and once again got into the rhythm, which had been interrupted by the meal and the percussionist's words. Do nothing, do nothing, get caught up in the swirl, he told himself, enter the whirlpool and go round with the water, fall into the chain reaction, into the surfaces of birds, decipher the signs, lay no obstacles before time, pull down a wall to let rhythm in and the pattern of the figure will emerge. He concentrated on making himself small in his chair, he felt the rhythm bear him off, he poked down deep inside, he trudged through snow, mud, volcanoes, he sighted herds of guanacos and vicuñas that had never been seen before and were careful about their shapes and signs, he caressed funeral urns and Indian mummies, he died at sea and got to know every shipwreck, he was resurrected and scaled mountains where he saw frightened gods fleeing and hiding, he caught a glimpse of the form and outline of a surface for humankind, and at last he raised his hand in the knowledge that from now on the rhythm would do everything. That's it, he said, dispersing the darkness; take him out to the patio and bring all our woven cloth.

The *ta ta*s were strong despite their schism with the *to to*s, but the *tu tu*s had absorbed the *ti ti*s and seemed to be in the majority.

'Same as ever,' Kico said. 'The *tu tu*s are always last but they're the ones that win. Must be the vowel they use to override storms.'

Old Aballay crossed the garden in a zigzag, and, blowing into his reed, was pursued by a cloud of *te te*s, which prudently moved off when he took up a new position and was approached by *to to*s. There was a spot by the garden's north wall that attracted *tu tu*s, but they stopped in their tracks when they saw *te te*s coming again. It seemed, however, that the old man had made contact with the centre, because now they all came on – though very timidly – and the old man disappeared in the thick of the bustling throng. Each bird now claiming its piece of thread, show a little patience, there's enough for everyone, in each little claw a slit like a buttonhole and a thread, all leading to Nabu. *Ta ta*s and *te te*s carry legs, *ti ti*s and *to to*s arms, *tu tu*s reserve the helm, the head, for themselves as they're the most expert, but in flight, when it comes to getting through a storm, each and every one will become *tu tu*s. Two of the compadre's fly-catchers arrive in an incredible state of nerves, bearing small slips of paper, strict orders, but they do not land, they're scared and turn tail in the face of the pandemonium. I'm sorry, compadre, you're always repeating yourself or getting here late, but you will agree that Nabu must leave this place our way. The *ta ta*s protest, you must hurry, they are the clocks of the rhythm, and there is no memory of their ever having been late. The cramped Aballays tie up the last few threads. Goodness, right on the nose, not one little table runner left.

Flying up, the birds unravel the table runners with the speed of creatures eager to migrate. The threads grow taut and the lengths of cloth disappear, leaving Nabu in the correct flight position.

'Is his name really Nabu?'

'A good question. You never know anything about people like him.'

Dressed as on the day he arrived, swimming without a stroke of his arms, his face expressionless, Nabu is a clapped-out machine that they lift into the air. He understands nothing when the old man tells him, pointing to the flock, that these birds were the funny notions the family had in their heads. The breeze brings tears to the percussionist's eyes. Belinda looks at him from the chimney, beside a balloon. Nabu flying overhead, above the weathercock, soon out of her sight. The cats are night blind. Belinda climbs down, purrs, butts into Julito, Julito waves a hand to say goodbye to the little drunkard. Birds fly off without entirely disclosing the secret of the figure. As if it were a handkerchief, the old man raises a thread on high, waving it, and bids Nabu farewell.

The worst thing for Nabu was to be borne off by a mechanism, something without ideas or feelings, a mechanism of animals, of the world, of blind things that couldn't be controlled, a mechanism no one had ever thought of before. The Cachimbas would have been preferable. Fear of physical danger, of the lack of skill of the towboats – these were another matter. Fear of this mechanism paralysed him. And he, as a percussionist, knew full well what the mechanism was. The branches of the hackberry tore his shirt and, thanks to his own efforts, he did not collide with the chimney. As he swung round, he came face to face with the cat, her eyes round, mechanical. I should have killed her on that first day, flashed through his mind. Turning her head, Belinda followed Nabu's flight with a look of utter indifference, and her bow grew yellow in the cool morning. Nabu had always been a blurry, dangerous bulk to her; and never more so than now, when he was flying off and she was already forgetting him. Her memory had exact limits. And she came down into the patio as if Nabu, now forgotten for ever, had never been there.

The percussionist took one last look back at her and the house as he was lifted beyond the garden wall. One of his eyes closed automatically as he took aim to kill her in his mind, but what he wanted to kill was a cold object, a weathercock in the shape of a cat.

His towboats had begun to climb, freeing him from the danger of lamp-posts, the factory tower, and the roofs of the jails, with their beacons which could have lighted up the night far beyond Hualacato. The balloon-filled town, the roads and roofs infested with Cachimbas, the bursting jails and wrecked control camps – it was all very quickly behind him now, how small Hualacato is. And off there in the distance, throngs of hunters running away, percussionists luckier than he managing to reach the country's borders. And still farther afield, towns under control, night-and-day pick-and-shovel work camps, men lifting their gaze to see birds and clouds overhead, see them get lost in the distance, and they lower their heads. In these towns there are neither balloons nor Cachimbas. Hunters roam the streets, their spiky hair blowing in the breeze, as they stroll about playing with their walking sticks and whistles. A stench reaches the birds from down below, a pulsating stench, particles of fear. With his experience, Nabu is quite familiar with the movement of such molecules, which begin to penetrate his old tiger's heart. Nabu, bidding farewell to everything, misses one final scene, which is blotted out by cloud cover. Far below in a village, a pride of lions corners a group of men, who are Mayan astronomers.

*Ti ti*s feel pain in their tarsi, *to to*s in their breastbones, and *te te*s in every bone in their bodies. *Tu tu*s, which command the flock, became aware of this by the sound of their feathers. There's a broken quill here, faulty rectrices there, and a certain lack of rhythm in the secondaries. It's the threads, say the *tu tu*s, who are strong but not very bright and are forever saying the obvious, things the whole flock already knows. Into the rain, into the rain, cry *te te*s and *ti ti*s. Rain falls to their right, and the *tu tu*s obediently change course, and the flock dives into the rain. Leg slits expand and claws drop their threads as if they were dropping a handkerchief. The first to be freed are the *tu tu*s; the last, the *ti ti*s.

Flying out of the rain they turn iridescent and feel incredibly light; now flying is pure delight. In the end, they all call themselves *tu tu*s. Those who'd been *ti ti*s have not the faintest idea of ever having been so, and they fly on out of habit, joyously, oblivious of whether they are bucking the wind or bringing up the rear of the flock, for that's where rhythm comes in – joy which is flight itself.

Once on their own flight paths, they no longer require

landmarks but keep a particular star in their memory – one that is fixed in the firmament. Below them now no jails or balloons or violent volumes, only the world as it is, turning, flying.

15

THEY WERE REMOVING the black pasteboard from the window panes when a smell of damp earth pervaded the house, whose doors and windows were now flung open on every side. It's raining in the hills, Sila said. In a minute or two it'll be raining in Hualacato. And they all ran to take their shoes off as the first big drops splattered on to the zinc roof. Radios and television sets that had been playing previously banned music interrupted their programmes to announce that there would be complete coverage of the rain for members of the public who for whatever reason were unable to get out of their homes.

The drops are crystal-clear and sparkling, like small toy worlds. It's raining, ladies and gentlemen, it's raining from heaven, said the news-readers, trite as ever. Television screens showed an old woman gazing up at the rain from her bed. Well, then, madame, what do you think of this rain? At a loss for words, the old woman blurted, it's just raining, from up there to down here. In the streets kids were getting wet, their little paper boats in readiness for the rising waters.

It was raining on Hualacato's crooked buildings, a field of maize was under water, and a south wind blew. Masons with plumb lines in their hands were waiting for clear skies so that the work of straightening houses could begin. The rain itself burst the banks of the channels built to divert and contain it, and now streams ran freely through roads and fields. People wading in the streets had to scramble up on to the pavements and seek shelter in entranceways as the flood poured down from the hills. But the most intoxicated remained outdoors, letting themselves be drenched by waters perfumed with herbs, and lovers came out to kiss in the rain.

Hualacateños dashed to and fro looking for missing persons, asking questions and looking, searching faces, have you seen this kid's parents, that old couple's small grandchildren, kidnapped with their parents, or the babies born in captivity of mothers who had been kidnapped during pregnancy. Sila ran along the street asking whether anyone had seen Aunt Francisquita with her Carlos. Coca knocked at Aunt Marcelina's door and nobody answered. Please, can you tell me if anybody's seen Aunt Céfira and her husband Lucho. No one had seen Yeyo, and Kico asked about Bocha. Each question was answered with another that asked about someone else. Kico made his way to Aunt Francisquita's to find the house buried under weeds. The doors were smashed, the empty house sheltered stray animals, and in the living room a horse browsed among broken coffee cups and shards of mirrors. Kico was near Yeyo's when the floodwaters burst and he had to take refuge in an old arched entranceway.

Hualacato and its swollen, parallel river-streets and people huddled on the pavements watching tree trunks and boulders flow past along with drowned animals and all the other things brought on this tide. On the Aballays' street the swirling waters were very noisy. Stones and bottles tumbled and collided on the tips of waves in a jumble of percussion instruments – big-bellied drums and small tabors, luxurious drum sets and lowly brushes – all bobbing alongside bony cymbals, kettledrums, and sistra, their distorted din merging with the groans of mournful gongs as they are struck by stones, according to the adjectives of a verbose news-reader.

'My goodness, so much going on,' said Coca, removing the last marks from the window panes on the street side.

On Aunt Francisquita's street, the first thing the tide brought was a vast black mass that never stopped flowing past. Thousands and thousands of black dogs formed a single mass, a wave of fangs and trained jaws, most of them alive and fighting each other, snapping their teeth and looking in vain for the river bank. And the roar of the water mixed with the sound of their barking and howling, with half-shaved heads bobbing in the swirl, the tufts of long hair surfacing and disappearing again amongst camera straps and broken blowguns – tourists on a river journey back to their own lands.

From their windows the Hualacateños bade them farewell, flinging paper cut-outs at them as if they were throwing flowers. They then caught sight of the swollen river's next big wave, bringing with it tons of warning notices, percussionists, and key-rings that sounded like wooden rattles – all under a rain of paper birds, butterflies, crabs, leaping frogs, herons, and carefully folded small fish thrown from the windows by an army of forced-labour experts in paper cut-outs.

On the next block some fat men went bobbing by. Still in their armchairs or behind desks or trailed by their secretaries, they sailed quietly down Aunt Céfira's street, studying their legal codes or accounting books or nervously tapping the buttons of their cordless phones. They were not many but having lots of furniture they took up several blocks' worth of river.

Only one fat man went down Yeyo's street. He was the fattest of all, and – being more intelligent – a foreigner. In his private plane, which bobbed up and down like a boat, he was carrying so many things he needed a whole river to himself. He had his jewels, shares, banks, mistresses, factories, guards, slot machines, chewing gum, soft drinks, cattle, and ships. He had an entire zoo, which was also his – tigers, bear cubs (which were blameless), giraffes stretching their necks out of the water, new-born panthers, young lions that still hadn't opened their eyes, and viruses and microbes that glowered from inside their glass jars. And bringing up the rear were his dead, in coffins with their gold handles at water level; close behind were other dead, of a station so low they didn't even have coffins. The flood also dragged by hidden cemeteries, and the news-reader – unable to find words for them all – overlooked a great number of things.

And Hualacato was resplendent under a pair of rainbows, looking like a town at the beginning of the world, ladies and gentlemen, like a living jewel, Hualacato.

The search went on when the floodwaters subsided. Have you seen Carlos, Lucho, Uncle Juanjo? No. You lot, have you seen Flaco, Tuco, or Aunt Delicia? Why wasn't Yeyo there? He never missed anything. Where's Yeyo? was all that had to be asked, and someone would say, you mean you haven't seen him? There he is. You turned your head, and Yeyo was always there.

They were counting up, and many were missing – at the bottom of dams, down mine shafts, in lime pits or the sea. Not counting those who'd fallen that same day, Cachimba among them.

I've never seen so many unfamiliar faces, said the old man, his chair pushing aside people who still splashed about in rain puddles. Let's look for them in their homes;

Aunt Francisquita's is quite near, said Coca. It's not worth it, Kico said; everybody's in the streets today. We'll find them some other time. Besides, it's getting cooler and we'd better start back. The kids are cold.

Words – like objects borne on the south wind – ran past people, and their heads nodded as the words swept past in waves, gusts rippling the heads of plants. People lifted their gaze to see words flying past like sheets of zinc or garments torn by a gale from clothes lines. The words *mine shaft* flew past like a dirty rag, followed by *two hundred*, which may have included any of those they were looking for. *At the bottom of the dam* went by, close together, like dead cats, and on their tail, like a whistling sound, the words *seven hundred*, where Aunt Francisquita could very well be. *Lime pits* flew past mixed with *three hundred*. *The sea* went by, and then there was silence. *Volunteers to dig* went by, and Kico made his way to where the words had come from.

A large group of men and women were excavating near where cries had been heard, an underground prison apparently connected with one of the factory's many levels, but among the maze of cellars no entrance could be found. The cellars were buried deep, and the volunteers felt the points of their picks strike a concrete vault. When cold chisels at last broke through, a stream of emaciated prisoners emerged, hobbling on their own convalescence. Has anyone seen Juanjo, Lucho, Yeyo, Uncle Carlos? As they came out of the cavern, the prisoners shot lizard-like looks at each person they saw but they did not open their mouths, and it was as if they had not heard. When the last face was out, Kico peered in and called. Aunt Francisquita! Aunt Céfira! He then stood at each corner, calling Uncle Juanjo, Aunt Marcelina, Yeyo, and when he got home his family were waiting and he asked, has anyone come, has anyone arrived? And the others replied, didn't you see anyone, didn't you find anyone? And a long time began to pass.

Well, said old Aballay, like everything else in the world birds have their particular truths. Either you know this or you observe it. These truths seem not to exist, which is why there's no thought about them. Perhaps such truths are not meant to be thought about but only approached. Analyse them and they die stillborn. The saviour was always trying to do that to us, always trying to use his powerful faculties to dissect us. But we weren't meant to be dissected and analysed – at least not that way. Birds don't think about the universe, they don't make representations of it. They've known the world since time began; they dwell in it, look at it, and, without violating it, they let it happen. All they want is to hitch themselves to the world's rhythm and allow it to go about its business, which is to continue within its existing pattern so that all of us can live in that pattern. The problem is that we don't yet know what that pattern is. The more we think about it the less we understand. This is the same thing as killing it.

The saviour was at the limits of his papers and of his own faculties, and he got mired down in them. Neither had anything to do with the world any longer; instead, they were the illusions of madness. People like him have a deep fear of the world and of life, and they can't see what is real. That's what gives rise to their hatred and madness.

The time I was made to live outdoors and thought I was finished, I mulled all these things over. That's why when we trapped the saviour I didn't want him killed, as so many others had been. Killing him would have been thinking him up, defining him, turning him into a symbol of something he was unworthy of. In spite of everything he took from us, I still feel the same. Of those we loved we have only photographs. Cholo, Yeyo, Aunt Francisquita, and so many others. Of Nabu, we wanted to keep his useless dog as a reminder of him, because if in a way we forgive him for living a life exempt from truths that were unknown to him, natural truths, this does not mean that we shall forget him. As everyone knows, these things are never forgotten.

Just as history cannot encompass time, which has no beginning and no end, none of Nabu's ideas can encompass man, for man does not stand still but like the birds he is a wanderer. In his wanderings he has left his mark on minerals, he has left his mummies in the snow or in caves, he has left his ideas in stone, he has left his wrecks in the sea. Like the birds, his paths were laid down for him when he began life. But those paths are full of obstacles that have to be removed so as not to encumber man, just as we once pulled down a wall so as not to block that path the birds knew by heart. To be removed so that, as is his habit, man can journey on for ever.

Word has been going round that we controlled Hualacato's cats and birds. We never controlled anything. All we did was look at the birds, which had always been a sort of habit. As for the cats, I don't think we ever looked at them; but we let them look at us, which amounts to the same thing. We always regarded them as extensions of ourselves; or ourselves as extensions of them, which again amounts to the same thing. So there's no need for either to think of the other.

I've told you everything I know, everything that was given me in the time I spent alone outdoors in what was our garden. I'm old now, and there are things I have forgotten, things that just slipped away because they're no longer worth remembering. There are many things I still want to forget. The hardship of what the percussionists call war has dulled my memory, and I mix things up. As for the lions trapped in the woods, for me the woods have become a kind of spider's web too. Maybe all this has been a sheer fantasy, what any prisoner thinks up when he's alone. Even so, it would be pointless to invent something that isn't in order that it should be – at least as long as this war with only one faction, this long percussionist soliloquy, goes on.

What's important with birds, besides looking at them, is to let them look at us. When we are still, they come to us of their own accord and not for the seed we offer them. That comes later, as a sign of friendship. They approach because we've become doors through which they can either come or go. That's why now that we have to remake Hualacato, we must make believe we're trapping lions. We have to put up a fence that's not a fence, so that time won't get trapped in it, for time is long and contains all our wanderings. Like the birds, time must be free to come and go. We must build a small door that isn't like a door, through which time and anything that hides will come in and go out. With such a device, perhaps we can trap those remaining woodland gods, who in their fear remain in hiding, still lingering out there in the mud and snow.

AFTERWORD

SOME YEARS AGO in the Argentine, a polemic erupted in which it was acrimoniously argued whether the country's literature from 1976 to 1983, the years of the brutal military dictatorship, had been written at home or in exile. One side, wrote Juan Carlos Martini, a novelist and chronicler of the debate,

> held that Argentine literature could only be written at home; the other, that it could only be written abroad. . . . Those in Argentina predicted that the exiles would never make their way into the local literary scene; those outside Argentina maintained that writers at home had but one of two choices – collaboration or self-censorship.

In the end the argument proved false, and the discussion petered out. The evidence was only too plain that the writing of the period in question was good (or bad) according to its authors' talent, imagination, and moral sense, wherever the three may have been exercised. Certainly, exile was no guarantee of quality. Argentine writers in forced or voluntary exile in Europe and the United States were sometimes easy prey to adulation and exploitation by correct-thinking Europeans and North Americans anxious to display solidarity and outrage at a time when the

Argentine nation was locked into sordid fratricidal blood-shed. In certain cases exile helped spurious, reprehensible, and even obscene writing to find its way into print abroad under the guise of committed literature. A number of reviewers outside Argentina were quick to attack any fiction that did not deal directly with the dark years of repression, while Argentine novelists and story-tellers after the return of democracy and freedom lamented that the rest of the world seemed to demand that they chronicle only torture, rape, brutality, and the disappearances.

While all of Argentina's masterworks of the last century – Esteban Echeverría's *Matadero*, Domingo F. Sarmiento's *Facundo*, José Mármol's *Amalia*, José Hernández's *Martín Fierro*, and Lucio Mansilla's *Excursión a los indios ranqueles* – were what today is known as committed writing, they were also works of literature. Alas, the same cannot be said of much work of the 1970s and 1980s, in spite of its passion and its stance against the regime. There is a certain uneasiness among some readers about the way torture, especially that of women, has often been revelled in, to the point of sensationalism and prurience. Paradoxically, the contemporary book that may one day rest alongside those nineteenth-century classics – and that makes any fictional treatment of the recent period of repression almost superfluous – was never meant to be literature. It is *Nunca Más*, the report of President Raúl Alfonsín's special commission into the fate of the twelve or so thousand Argentines who disappeared off the streets, a book that one critic has said 'describes in detail almost unbearable to read the system of licensed sadism the military rulers of Argentina created in their country from 1976 to 1979 . . .'

A more fruitful discussion about the fiction of the 1980s would have focused on the nature and quality, not the place of origin, of literary production as well as on the myriad issues raised by any imaginative writing about cataclysmic historical events in which authors take sides. Or by any imaginative writing in the midst of cataclysmic historical events that chooses to ignore them. Comparisons and contrasts with the rich period during and after the Rosas dictatorship a hundred and fifty years ago would perhaps have been more pertinent. In any case, the conclusion reached by Martini would have been the same: 'An Argentine writer has no choice but to write Argentine novels, wherever he lives and whatever his circumstances, however much we may or may not like it.'

Where do Daniel Moyano and *The Flight of the Tiger* fit into all this? Curiously – emblematically, almost – Moyano was to write his novel twice, first in Argentina's poor western province of La Rioja, where he lived until 1976, then again, several years later, in exile in Madrid, where the book was originally published in 1981. The writing of the novel is a story in itself. Along with other writers and intellectuals of La Rioja, Moyano was rounded up and jailed shortly after Argentina's military takeover on 24 March 1976. His compelling account of his incarceration, untold until almost a dozen years later, appears as 'The White Wall and the Spiders' in Andrew Graham-Yooll's *After the Despots*. After twelve days, Moyano was released. Typical of the military justice of the period (if the oxymoron is permitted), he never found out why he was jailed; nor did he ever learn why he was let go. The experience, the fear, was so searing, however, that he lost no time in packing up his house, gathering his wife and children, and emigrating to freedom in Spain, which they reached on 8 June. In an earlier conversation with Graham-Yooll, Moyano said that he had drafted *The Flight of the Tiger* in La Rioja but that

When I had been jailed there my family buried the manuscript in the garden. Had the army searched my house and found it they would never have let me go. A priest who had been to my house said, 'Make that manuscript disappear.' So it stayed buried in the garden; it was my only copy. Here in Spain I undertook to reconstruct the novel from scratch. When I went back to La Rioja, a fig tree in the garden had been cut down and a lawn and swimming pool had been put in. Who knows what ever happened to my original script.

The novel is an allegorical tale of a military-style take-over and occupation of a village in the Andes 'lost somewhere amid the cordillera, the sea, and adversity.' Nowhere in the book is Argentina mentioned, for by the time Moyano reconstructed the novel in Madrid – incorporating into it several details of his nightmarish ordeal in detention in La Rioja, where at one point he and his fellow prisoners were made to stand before a white wall counting tiny spiders as they waited to be shot – he was interested in a truth that went beyond the political confines of his own country. (Does the January 1994 revolt in the Mexican state of Chiapas not uphold Moyano's thesis?) 'I admire Borges and love you,' Moyano once told fellow novelist Julio Cortázar, 'but in his language the Mexican writer Rulfo says more to me.' Here in the Hualacato of his novel is the beginning of the author's identification, pursued in subsequent fiction, with a Latin America that is not Europeanised Buenos Aires but Andean, with pre-Columbian roots.

Eschewing naturalism, in *The Flight of the Tiger* Moyano has invented a completely original story, setting, and characters. Mercifully, the book is not one more chronicle of peasants struggling to overcome tyrants. From the opening pages, we are matter-of-factly plunged into a unique world in which percussionists come riding in on their tigers, time and crops are taken over, rain no longer falls, and buildings sag under unimaginable winds. The percussionists (or in their terms, 'saviours') are the town's invaders and occupiers, who are out to cleanse the village of Hualacato of subversive thought. In everyday terms, call them what you will – baddies, storm-troopers, Fascists, the military (or paramilitary), a latter-day *mazorca*. For a professional musician like Moyano, a novelist and journalist who also taught music and was a violinist in a string quartet and string orchestra, what better name for a faceless sinister horde who abhor silence and exhort the Hualacateños to make every sort of noise, racket, clatter, din, and unearthly clangour? Interestingly enough, we meet only one of them, the nondescript Nabu, who holds the eight-strong Aballay family under house arrest.

The book has its difficulties but these are easily overcome. For English-speaking readers, the typically Andean two-syllable names of the main characters – Cholo and Coca (the mother and father), Kico and Sila (the teenage brother and sister), Tite (the young brother dead years earlier at the age of four) – are unfamiliar and at first hard to sort out. Confusing too is the fact that two of the three youngest children are never named and barely glimpsed. The wheelchair-ridden grandfather, in some ways the tale's protagonist, is known only by his odd surname, Aballay; and, not least, one of the key presences in the book is the family cat, Belinda.

Nor is any of these central characters ever described. Physical description is reserved for the story's rich substratum of secondary characters, relatives and friends, whom we come to know through a ragtag boxful of old snapshots. Although we never meet them, the others weave their way in and out of the book and are virtually ever-present.

Paradoxically, we get a far more intimate look into their lives than we do into those of the Aballay family.

In ways the book is a novel of voices. Speakers, often unidentified and sometimes seemingly unidentifiable, constantly change, and the conventional indicators – punctuation, indention, quotation marks – are frequently omitted, so that only by concentration will the reader work out whose words we are hearing. There are only words, or snatches of speech, or overlapping conversations on which we eavesdrop. Added to this, tenses too shift between present and past, just as sentences shift from first- to third-person narration. Time, as announced on page one, is also thrown out of the window, and there is no way of knowing in what space the novel unfolds. Here and there, perhaps, are dreamlike hints of several years. And all the while, in keeping with the humble background and unreflective nature of the characters and the phantasmagoric, hallucinatory experiences they undergo, the Aballays are constantly thinking aloud and engaging in imaginary dialogues with their interrogator in which they project both what Nabu will ask them and what they will reply. This is thought in terms of human interaction, not abstractions. Into their true and feigned innocence, confusion, and lack of understanding come stabs of evasiveness, prevarication, and efforts of peasant craft and cunning. Very soon all attempts at language in the brusque, McCarthy-style cross-questioning (any United States citizen of a certain age will be reminded of the ugly, hateful 1950s un-American shibboleths spewed out by rote to determine un-Americanism: 'Are you now, or have you ever been, a member of the Communist Party?' and 'Do you believe in the overthrow of the government by force and violence?') disintegrate into high-sounding verbal gibberish.

For the rest, once the reader accepts the story's surface

strangeness (the role of origami in the plot, tourists with blowguns and punk hair-dos, the Byzantine rules that govern the Aballays' confinement, amongst a score of other bizarre details) and begins to see the satire and black humour that underlie many of the novel's random vignettes, the book becomes a romp. Moyano was renowned among his friends as an oral story-teller. One glimpse into 'The White Wall and the Spiders', which Andrew Graham-Yooll recorded on tape in 1988 and which required virtually no editing, reveals the author's gifts to the full. In *The Flight of the Tiger*, the grandfather too tells entertaining stories, and a number of his enigmatic tales are woven into the novel, sometimes only tangentially. One has to do with the trapping of a mountain lion up a tree, another with Eskimos and polar bears and the transmission of life, a third with the first time old Aballay views the sea. Occasionally these stories are symbolic, at other times they seem almost pointless asides. But that we are gripped by them, that it may be best not to puzzle their meaning too closely, is enough.

There is one whole chapter dealing with torture, but Moyano is too intelligent and sensitive to linger on the details of what Nabu and his instruments do to the old patriarch. Another Argentine novelist, Humberto Costantini, wrote from exile in Mexico in 1979 that

> it is impossible to describe torture from the victim's point of view. Those attempts I am familiar with always seemed phoney, literary, and, above all, irreverent.
>
> Nor is it possible to describe absolute pain. Any metaphor comes across as contrived, any objective account turns out wanting or weak, any serious attempt to get inside the victim becomes senseless, presumptuous . . .
>
> The truth of the matter is that faced with describing absolute pain, unrelieved pain, one can only remain silent.

> I mean respectfully silent and not try to do what is beyond
> human capacity – to put oneself in the skin of someone
> who is undergoing such pain and suffer it with him.

It would appear that Moyano wholly subscribed to Costantini's wise dictum.

Moyano has related that, between the first publication of his previous novel *The Devil's Trill* in Buenos Aires in 1974 (the book was later revised and reissued in Madrid in 1988; the English version, which appeared in a translation by Giovanni Pontiero, is based on the Buenos Aires text) and the publication of *The Flight of the Tiger* in 1981, seven years passed when he was unable to write. Certainly the feeling we get reading the novel is that it was composed at white-hot speed. Not every page is polished, and passages are sometimes merely sketched; in places this is further reduced almost to telegraphic jottings, as if the author meant to flesh them out later but never returned to the task. And yet, make no mistake, chapter by chapter the novel is highly organised and tightly constructed.

The conclusion comes at a dizzying pace and, if anything, is even more wildly imaginative than all that has come before. Here, with the deliverance of Hualacato, we are treated to a mixture of broad humour and pathos. There is one particularly savage and colourful bit when rain turns the streets into swollen rivers and Moyano revels in a Dantesque catalogue of what comes bobbing along on the rushing torrent, including an obese plutocrat in his private plane, carrying 'his jewels, shares, banks, mistresses, factories, guards, slot machines, chewing gum, soft drinks, cattle, and ships.' Spared a trial by the generous Aballays, Nabu is nonetheless ingeniously dispatched in a climax of Biblical inspiration, complete with its epic flood and full-scale gloria. What brings down the infamous percussionists? In Nabu's own words, 'blind things that couldn't be controlled, a mechanism no one had ever thought of before'. To the Aballays it was their dreams, something they 'could touch without feeling fear', something that belonged to them and that Nabu could not get at. Succinctly, in 1845, Sarmiento placed at the head of his *Facundo* these words by a French writer: *On ne tue point les idées*. You never kill ideas.

From the appearance of his first book in 1960, Daniel Moyano published six volumes of short stories (not counting two others of selected stories) and six novels. Born in Buenos Aires in 1930, from the age of four he grew up near Córdoba, where he was a school mate of Che Guevara, with whom he once stole peaches in the garden of the exiled Spanish composer Manuel de Falla. Moyano's mother, who died when he was seven, was a Protestant; her family had emigrated to Brazil from Piedmont, in Italy. In 1960, he went to La Rioja, where his father's family had lived and where he worked in journalism. Moyano obtained Spanish nationality in 1981. On his death, in Madrid, in July 1992, he left an unpublished novel, *Dónde estás con tus ojos celestes*, and an unpublished volume of short stories whose themes embrace the world of music.

Norman Thomas di Giovanni
Gunn, Goodleigh, Devon